THE PORTSMOUTH MURDERS

A gripping crime thriller full of twists

PAULINE ROWSON

The Solent Murder Mysteries book 1

Originally published as
Tide of Death

JOFFE BOOKS

Revised edition 2022
Joffe Books, London
www.joffebooks.com

First published by Fathom in Great Britain in 2006
as *Tide of Death*

Cover art by Nick Castle and
Dee Dee Book Covers in collaboration

ISBN: 978-1-80405-059-0

For Bob

AUTHOR'S NOTE

This novel is set in Portsmouth, Hampshire, on the south coast of England. Residents of and visitors to Portsmouth must forgive the author for using her imagination and poetic licence in changing the names of places, streets and locations. This novel is entirely a work of fiction. The names, characters, businesses, locations and incidents portrayed in it are entirely the work of the author's imagination. Any resemblance to actual persons, living or dead, events or locations is entirely coincidental.

Please note this book is set in the early 2000s, when technology was somewhat different.

ONE

Wednesday 7 a.m.

Andy Horton stared at the body. The face was almost obliterated. Blood had seeped onto the pebbled beach, dark red, staining the stones around the man's head. Bottle-green seaweed was wrapped around his ankles and he was naked; his arms were outstretched, the palms facing upward, fingers curled.

Horton averted his eyes and lowered his head over his torso, trying to catch his breath from his run. His stomach churned at the shock of such a gruesome discovery. It wasn't that he had never seen a dead body before, or a violent death; on the contrary, in his job they were all too plentiful. No, it was the unexpectedness of running into one that temporarily unnerved him. He usually arrived after some other poor sod had found it. And he'd got out of practice; eight months away from the sharp end had softened him.

He straightened up, wiping the sweat from his face, and stared around but all he could see was fog and all he could hear was the mournful boom of the foghorns in the Solent calling to one another like long lost giants.

He punched a number into his mobile. Why did this have to happen today of all days, only his second day back on duty after his suspension? But sod's law always prevailed; either that or God had a wicked sense of humour, and if He did then He couldn't be God, could He? But maybe he should be grateful to the corpse. This would give him a chance to show his colleagues that he hadn't lost his touch.

'DI Horton, is the DCI in?'

'No, sir, he's at the hospital.'

'He's ill?' Horton asked surprised.

'No, sir, it's PC Evans. He was stabbed last night.'

'Christ! Is he all right?' Poor Evans, the station joker, only two months away from retirement and counting the days.

'He's in intensive care. But they think he'll pull through.'

'Well thank God for that,' Horton replied with feeling, picturing poor Maureen Evans' face.

He quickly relayed the news of his discovery on Portsmouth's beach and settled down to wait. He knew it wouldn't be long. He took another look at the body. Who was he? What had he done to warrant such a violent death? Over the next couple of days they'd begin to find out. The team would be assembled, people questioned, statements taken and, hopefully, the victim identified. The investigative machine would swiftly gear itself into action and he was determined to play a central role in it. He was still a good cop, despite the Lucy Richardson episode, which had cost him his position in the Special Investigations Department and earned him an eight-month suspension.

Impatiently he glanced at his watch, and as he did, four uniformed officers emerged from the fog armed with tape and bollards. He instructed two of them to seal off the beach to the east by the cruising association slipway and the other two to cordon off the area to the west below the old gunnery site. He looked up to see DCI Uckfield ploughing across the stones towards him. Horton pulled himself up. He couldn't afford to foul up on this one.

'You're out of condition, Steve.' He smiled at the man who had helped him get back into CID. 'Too much time sitting behind that desk.'

'Tell me about it. You look disgustingly fit.'

'Well I've had the time,' Horton replied caustically. They'd joined the force together eighteen years ago and had been good friends since, but for the last three years, while on secondment to Special Investigations, Horton had seen little of Uckfield. They began walking towards the body.

Horton said, 'What happened with Evans?'

'Fortunately the knife missed the main arteries. I was just visiting the scene-of-crime, a house in Hemmings Road, just off the seafront, when I got the call saying you'd found a body. Evans and PC Kate Somerfield were called out by neighbours who were complaining about the noise from a party. Somerfield went inside to tell the kids to turn the volume down and Evans went round the back of the house. She didn't know he'd been stabbed until a few minutes later.'

'Did they get him?'

'Who said it was a him?'

'Usually is.'

Uckfield sniffed and retrieved a wooden toothpick from the depths of his jacket pocket. 'The little scumbag got away but we'll get him. You can bet your pension on that.'

I don't think my pension's the safest thing to bet on, Horton thought, given his history.

Uckfield manipulated the toothpick in his mouth and stared down at the body just the other side of the blue and white tape. Horton had seen quite enough already but he looked again. The grey hairs on the slender frame and the slackness of the skin told him their victim was middle-aged, probably late fifties. He was a tall man, about six foot two.

'The body is oddly . . .'

'Positioned?' offered Horton.

'Why like that as if he's on a cross? Can't have been washed up in that position.'

'No. And he's been placed, or was killed, just above the tide line, see?' Horton pointed to the line of seaweed that delineated the height of the last tide. 'He's not wet and there's no decomposition so he can't have been here long. This isn't a popular spot for sunbathers, though it is sometimes used by nudists.'

'He's in good company then.' Uckfield stared down at the naked body. 'Could he be one of them?'

'A nudist sunbather, you mean?' Horton shrugged. 'No idea, but if he was then where are his clothes? They should be beside him along with his other belongings like his wallet and watch.'

'Perhaps he left them in his car?'

'In the car park? A couple of hundred yards away? He'd have to be some kind of pervert to walk here in the nude.'

'It's been known,' Uckfield said cynically, replacing the toothpick in his pocket.

'Did you see a car parked?'

'OK, so the killer stripped him and took away the poor bugger's clothes after smashing his face to a pulp. It's obvious why.'

'To delay identification.'

'Then thank God he didn't hack off the hands.'

Yes, and thank God for DNA, Horton thought. 'His face could have been beaten by the killer in an act of fury rather than to deliberately delay identification, and the clothes taken away as an afterthought.'

Uckfield lifted one shoulder in a semi-shrug. 'Possible.'

'I can't see a weapon unless our killer used a large stone to batter him. It could be any one of those around his head.'

'We'll get a search going but my guess is it won't do much good. If our killer's got any sense then whatever he used will be way out there somewhere.' Uckfield pointed in the direction of the sea. 'When was high tide?'

'Just before midnight.'

Uckfield rubbed his nose and looked thoughtful. 'Could he have been brought in by boat?'

'In last night's fog? If he was then whoever did it would have to be a very good sailor.'

'But it's not impossible, is it, with GPS and a tender?'

Uckfield was a competent sailor like him but Horton wouldn't like to have done it. 'No, just very difficult.'

More officers had appeared and Uckfield stepped away from the body as a large polythene tent was erected over it. Horton fell into step beside him as they moved down to the water's edge. The fog obscured the shores of Hayling Island across the narrow entrance to Langstone harbour. Horton could hear the slow beat of the waves as they washed gently onto the shore. As the sun grew in strength it would burn off the fog to reveal another stifling hot August day. It would be difficult keeping the area sealed off; the sooner they could move the body and get the scene-of-crime team in, the better. He felt his pulse quicken at the thought of the intense activity ahead. The clock had begun ticking and the race was on to find a killer before the trail grew cold. This was what he had missed.

Uckfield's voice broke through his thoughts. 'Any idea who he is?'

'No. Why do you ask?' Horton was instantly on guard. What did Uckfield mean? He tensed, scrutinising his friend's face but Uckfield's expression gave nothing away. Horton forced himself to relax, but his fists were tightly balled. 'You can't think I've got anything to do with this?'

'Of course not.'

Horton didn't like the slight pause Uckfield had left before answering, nor the fact that he wouldn't look him in the eye. Perhaps he was being over sensitive. 'Look, I found a body, by accident. It happens.'

'I know.' Uckfield held up his hands in capitulation. 'It's just awkward you finding it, after that business with Lucy Richardson. Do you always run this way?' His casual manner didn't fool Horton.

'Not always,' he replied, tight-lipped. Uckfield nodded and fell silent.

Horton took a deep breath and tried to get his emotions under control. 'I couldn't sleep,' he said, tersely. 'I decided to run the length of the seafront to Old Portsmouth and back again. I saw what I thought was a shop dummy on the beach and ran up to take a closer look. I found him.' Slowly finger-by-finger he unfurled his fists, mentally counting them off as he did. Would everyone always regard him with suspicion?

'You'd better get off home and change before the media come sticking their noses in the trough. Ask Sergeant Trueman to run a check on missing persons and then deal with Evans' stabbing. I've left the file on your desk,' Uckfield continued.

Steve Uckfield may have put in a good word to get him reassigned to CID, but now it was clear that he didn't trust him. It hurt and stung him to resentment. Horton wanted to protest but could see from Steve's expression that it wouldn't do any good. His own expression must have betrayed his feelings though.

Uckfield said, 'I'm doing you a favour.'

'It doesn't feel like it.'

'You're still on the team, Andy, but it's best if you get away now and stay clear until the media interest dies down. You know what they're like.'

He did all too well. 'OK,' he reluctantly agreed.

Uckfield turned away to talk to the head of the scene-of-crime team making it perfectly clear their conversation was over. Horton's fury was tainted with disappointment as he jogged eastwards along the beach barely acknowledging the officers who passed him. He felt like an outsider in an organisation that had once been the only family he'd had until Catherine and Emma. And now he'd lost them.

His mind returned to that surveillance operation, as it often did. He'd been working in the Special Investigations Department, on a joint operation with the Vice Squad, watching Alpha One, a prestigious, men only health club and gym at Oyster Quays, a popular waterfront development of offices and shops overlooking the entrance to Portsmouth Harbour. Its owner, Colin Jarrett, was suspected of running a prostitution ring and escort agency and using the club as a centre for distributing pornography to members for gain. Membership was by invitation only and the list highly secret. There was no point raiding the place because they needed proof and they needed to know how the pornographic material was getting into the country. Horton had been designated to get close to one of the girls working there, Lucy Richardson, and find a way inside.

It had been easy arranging to bump into her coming out of Alpha One and to ask her for a drink — too easy looking back on it. He had been too keen and too impatient to get a result. A drink had led to a meal and then to a rendezvous at the Holiday Inn Express. He hadn't believed then that she had known he was a copper, but now he realised he had been too blind and stupid to see he was being set up. Until then he had always thought of himself as a good policeman, but it just showed how wrong he could be.

The car park was cordoned off and almost overflowing with police cars. The mobile incident unit was being manoeuvred into place. Uckfield may be shutting him out physically but that didn't mean he couldn't think about the body on the beach and contribute his ideas. He'd make them heard whether Uckfield liked it or not.

There were no houses here, just the marina opposite where he lived on his boat. The cruising association clubhouse was to his right and bordering it to the west was the wide grassy expanse of Fort Cumberland, which was fenced off. It was a good spot to murder someone or plant a body.

A car horn tooted and a dark blue Vauxhall swept through the small crowd of commuters from the Hayling Ferry who had gathered to see what all the excitement was about. Soon the cream of the south's journalists would be breaking out all over the place like a nasty rash. Uckfield was right, though Horton was reluctant to admit it, he couldn't face them, especially dressed as he was in his running gear.

He waited for DC Walters to heave himself out of the car and waddle towards him. His ill-fitting suit was crumpled and shiny with wear and his appearance was in such sharp contrast to the trim DC Marsden that it made Horton think of Laurel and Hardy. Only this was no laughing matter.

Walters took a large handkerchief from his trouser pocket and wiped the beads of perspiration from his forehead.

'Where's Sergeant Cantelli?' Horton asked.

'Overslept, Inspector. Phoned in to say he'd be late.'

That wasn't like Cantelli. Horton had known Barney almost as long as he'd known Steve Uckfield and he had worked with Cantelli in CID for twelve years before being posted to other departments. In all that time Cantelli had never been late for work. He hoped he wasn't ill. Or perhaps concern for his wife, Charlotte, or one of their five offspring, had given the sergeant a restless night and caused him to oversleep.

Horton's mind returned to the case. How long would Uckfield keep him away from the investigation? If he was only going to be allowed to work on routine stuff — not that the Evans stabbing was routine — then there was surely no point in staying in the force, except for one thing. Only by being on the inside could he hope to find out who had set him up and why. With that came the chance of salvaging his reputation as a police officer and detective, and the chance of resuscitating his failed marriage.

As he punched in the pontoon security number a voice hailed him. It was Eddie, one of the marina staff.

'What's going on?' Eddie jerked his head in the direction of the beach. 'I saw all the police cars.'

Horton told him briefly. 'I don't suppose you saw or heard anything unusual last night?'

Eddie shook his head. 'Only the foghorns.'

'What time did you come on duty?'

'Eight o'clock.'

'Any cars in the car park then?'

The small man's bronzed, wrinkled face puckered up with concentration. 'I didn't really look.'

'Never mind.' Horton made to turn away.

'Oh, Andy, I nearly forgot in all the excitement. Post for you.'

Horton took the envelope with some trepidation. His stomach tightened at the sight of the red franking ink that bore the name of Catherine's solicitors. He had been dreading this. He knew it might come but he hadn't wanted to believe it. There was still time, he told himself, just as he had been telling himself for eight months. Time for him and Catherine to be reunited. But the record had got stuck and he'd done nothing about it. And now this. His fingers gripped the envelope. If he ripped it up . . . if he pretended it had never arrived . . .

He flung it onto the bunk, collected his towel and toilet bag and headed for the marina showers. The letter was still there when he returned — no good fairy had spirited it away. He stuffed it into the pocket of his trousers along with a tie and glanced in the small mirror hanging beside his berth. Christ, he looked awful. Why would Catherine still want him? There were bags under his eyes the size of suitcases and the tiny lines stretching from their edges made him look at least twenty years older than his thirty-eight.

He unpinned the photograph of his daughter, Emma, beside the mirror. Her impish grin and big brown eyes stared out at him. Dressed proudly in her school uniform she looked younger than her eight years and so vulnerable. A pain stabbed at his heart; his arms longed to hold her, to feel her little hands clasped around the back of his neck, to hear her giggle. His stomach tensed and it was all he could do to breathe.

His mobile phone rang. It was Cantelli.

'The DCI wants us to follow up on Evans' stabbing. You know about that? Damn tough, on poor Brian.' Cantelli's usually bright tone softened. 'I'll come and collect you.'

Horton put Emma's photograph back where it belonged, locked up his small yacht, *Nutmeg,* and was waiting at the entrance to the marina when Cantelli showed up ten minutes later. The sergeant looked as tired as he did. His almost black eyes were bloodshot and as if to confirm Horton's diagnosis Cantelli yawned.

'Kids keeping you awake?' Horton grunted. He had to take his anger and frustration out on someone and neither Uckfield, nor Colin Jarrett, the man he held responsible for his wrecked marriage, was there.

'You could say that.' Cantelli indicated right. 'I see we're not invited to the party then?'

'I know why I'm on the outside but what about you?'

Cantelli shrugged. A couple of minutes later he pulled up at the traffic lights and reached for a packet of chewing gum in the space by the hand brake. He offered the packet across to Horton, who declined. The lights changed. Cantelli turned right and headed away from the case.

'So tell me about Evans,' Horton said, trying to shake off his disgruntled mood. It wasn't easy, but neither was it Cantelli's fault so he shouldn't take it out on him.

'The boy who was holding the party was brought in for questioning but he's a juvenile, fifteen, and he was pilled up to his eyeballs so they didn't get anything out of him last night. His parents are on holiday, they've been contacted and they're on their way back. They fly in from Spain later this morning.'

'He's a bit young to have been left on his own.'

'There's an older brother, nineteen, but he was sleeping over at his girlfriend's. Social services have been informed and the drug squad are involved. Some kids gave their names but most were too out of it and others quickly scarpered.'

'So when can we interview this boy?'

'John Westover. This afternoon, one o'clock. Brian's still unconscious.'

'So not much point going to the hospital.'

'No. I've got a PC there who will call us the moment he comes round.'

Cantelli was heading out of the city. Horton was surprised. They were going in the wrong direction for the station and they'd already passed Hemmings Road, the scene of Evans' stabbing.

'Where are we going?'

'To see a lady.'

Horton raised his eyebrows. 'What lady?'

'The one who thinks the body you tripped over this morning is her husband.'

Horton's heart gave a lift. A shiver of excitement ran through him. He couldn't be this lucky, or could he? 'Go on,' he said, hardly daring to hope.

'She hasn't seen him since Friday when he went out on his boat,' Cantelli explained, as they crawled their way through the rush hour traffic. The fog was billowing off the shore to their right making the driving more hazardous than normal and the traffic slower.

'That's five days ago; it's taken her a long time to report him missing. Who is he?'

'Roger Thurlow, runs a marketing and public relations agency, at Oyster Quays.'

Cantelli gave him a swift glance, which Horton interpreted as a warning, but a friendly one. Stay away from Alpha One. From Barney Cantelli, Horton could take it. He was the only one who had believed him when he said he hadn't slept with Lucy Richardson let alone raped her. And that wasn't just out of gratitude for keeping Barney's nephew out of prison five years ago. Barney knew how much Horton's family meant to him and that he would never have risked losing them.

'Why does she think the body I found on the beach is her husband? Or is that just your opinion?'

'The description Mrs Thurlow gave fits: late fifties, slim build, greying hair, on the tall side. And, just before she phoned, I took a call from the Marine Support Unit. They were called out to a deserted motorboat this morning stranded on the East Winner bank. And guess who the owner is?'

'Roger Thurlow.'

'Yep.'

'Still doesn't mean it's the victim.' Horton stared out of the insect-spattered window. Could it be though? It sounded remarkably like it. He'd been given a lead or rather Cantelli had and Horton was damn sure he was going to follow it up. 'How come you put the two together so quickly?'

Cantelli shrugged and said casually, 'I was walking through reception and heard the desk clerk take the call.'

'Uckfield doesn't know we're going to see her?'

'No.' Cantelli smiled and there was a smug look on his lean, dark face. Horton thought it was good to be working with Cantelli again. 'I'm not sure if the desk clerk heard me say I was on my way to interview her and tell the DCI we might have an ID.'

'Then I'd better tell him.'

'Before you do, Andy, there's something else you ought to know.'

There always was with Cantelli. 'Yes?'

'Thurlow lives at Briarly House, on the outskirts of Redvins.'

That was where Uckfield lived. Redvins was a small village eight miles to the east of Portsmouth and four miles to the north of the coastal village of Emsworth. Horton recalled Uckfield's words, 'Do you know who he is?' *He* didn't but the DCI might.

He called Uckfield, feeling fired up. God had smiled on him and given him a chance, or rather Cantelli had. He wasn't going to let this slip through his fingers. When Uckfield came on the phone, Horton quickly explained the situation. Uckfield didn't sound too happy about them going to see Mrs Thurlow but there wasn't much he could do.

'I'm waiting for the pathologist to arrive,' Uckfield growled. 'Call me as soon as you've finished interviewing her. I've got to brief the Super and I'm giving a press statement at ten.'

Horton rang off. 'Seems like we just gate crashed the party.'

TWO

By the time they turned into the long gravel drive and pulled up outside Briarly House, the sun had burnt away the fog.

'Nice place,' Cantelli said, climbing out and stretching his hairy forearms into his jacket. 'Can't be short of a bob or two.'

Horton gazed up at the brick and flint period thatched cottage. He wasn't so sure. The house looked neglected, the thatch was yellowing and loose in places, the wooden window frames in need of replacing, and the paint on the heavy wooden door chipped and faded. It was in sharp contrast to the gardens either side of the drive where the grass, although showing signs of suffering from the long hot August, was nevertheless neatly cut. The borders teamed with colourful fuchsias and at either side of the door stood two standard fuchsia plants, a riot of pinks and purples.

It took several stout knocks, a call through the black iron letterbox and a finger pressed permanently on a brass bell, which Horton suspected didn't work, before they got a response. Cantelli had been about to set off round one side of the house in search of its owner when the door opened.

'Mrs Thurlow?' Horton asked.

'Yes?' she replied guardedly, restraining a golden retriever who looked more welcoming than his mistress.

Cantelli eyed the dog warily, as Horton quickly made the introductions and flashed his warrant card.

'I'm sorry I was in the garden. I must say I didn't expect anyone so promptly. I've not long telephoned.'

She was quite a handsome woman, Horton thought, with good bone structure and cool green eyes. He guessed she was about mid-fifties but her tanned and weathered face made her look older. Her grey hair was untidy and she was dressed in shorts and a faded T-shirt that had smears of earth on it.

She stepped back and Horton dipped his head as he entered. The dog barked. Cantelli hesitated.

'It's all right he won't hurt you,' she assured him.

'I've heard that one before,' Cantelli muttered, following her into the coolness of the hall where she let go of the dog's collar. Horton smiled as the animal pointedly ignored him and sniffed around Cantelli.

'He likes you,' Horton said.

'Glad someone does.' Cantelli reached out a hand and tentatively patted the animal's head. Satisfied, the dog trotted off ahead of his mistress and Cantelli heaved a sigh of relief.

Inside there was the same air of neglect as outside. The house smelt musty, the parquet flooring looked in need of polishing, the rugs had been worn almost to a thread, the floral wallpaper was dated and faded and the paintwork yellow rather than cream. She led them through an untidy kitchen that hadn't seen an upgrade for years judging by its solid oak cabinets and Aga, and into a ramshackle conservatory crammed with fuchsia plants.

'Please.' She waved them into seats and Horton picked up a pile of magazines, placed them on the wicker table and lowered himself warily onto a wooden chair that looked as if it could hardly cope with the weight of a child let alone twelve and a half stone of solid muscle.

Although the rather grubby blinds were half drawn and the door open, the heat was intense and within seconds Horton could feel his shirt sticking to his back. Cantelli's dark curly hair looked wet with sweat and he wriggled uncomfortably easing his jacket open. Horton was glad he had left his in the car. Mrs Thurlow seemed immune to the clawing heat; there wasn't a single bead of sweat on her brow.

'I suppose you've come about Roger,' she said offhandedly. Horton thought she might just have well been speaking about an old umbrella she'd left on a bus rather than her husband.

'I understand that you haven't seen him since Friday morning, is that correct?'

'Yes, he went sailing straight from work.'

'And he hasn't called you since then?'

'No. Here, Bellman.' She clicked her fingers and the dog left the bowl of water he'd been slurping from and trotted around to her side where he flopped onto the quarry-tiled floor, panting heavily.

Horton saw Cantelli give the dog an envious look before retrieving the small, stubby pen from behind his right ear and a notebook from his jacket pocket. Horton wouldn't have minded a drink himself but clearly they weren't going to be offered one.

'Is that usual?' Cantelli asked.

Mrs Thurlow looked at him blankly for a moment and Horton elaborated. 'He doesn't call you when he's away on his boat?'

'Oh, no.' She sounded surprised as if he'd suggested something improper.

'When were you expecting him back?' he asked, he hoped reassuringly. He needn't have bothered; it was wasted on her.

She shrugged. 'When he showed up. I'm not my husband's keeper and he's not mine.'

'Surely he gave some indication?' Horton injected an element of incredulity into his voice. She flushed slightly. Her eyes darted between him and Cantelli, betraying the first sign of unease.

'Look, I really didn't want to bother you, Inspector, but Mrs Stephens, his secretary, insisted. I am sure there's a perfectly good reason why my husband has not returned. Mrs Stephens is a little overprotective when it comes to Roger.'

And you're not, thought Horton watching her closely. She held his eyes. If she read his thoughts and was embarrassed by them she didn't show it. She lifted the coffee cup in front of her and took a sip, then pulled a face. Horton guessed it had grown cold.

'You don't go out on the boat with him?' he asked, lightly.

She answered as if he'd personally insulted her. 'Certainly not.'

He wondered if her terseness was a cover for shyness, or guilt perhaps. He got the impression she didn't really care that much for her husband but that didn't mean she had killed him. The body on the beach might not be Thurlow at all, although in a way he hoped it was. It would give him a head start in the investigation.

He'd seen both a radio and television in her kitchen so sooner or later she was bound to hear the news and might make the connection, better if he told her now. That way he could get something of Thurlow's and make a quick identification. Time was critical and he didn't mean purely in terms of tracking down the killer while the trail was still warm. He couldn't see her going into hysterics. She wasn't the type. Self-contained was perhaps how he might describe her; cold is what others might say. It was a description that had been levelled at him but self-containment, he knew, was a protection against being hurt.

'Don't you like sailing?' he asked.

'No I don't, Inspector. I can't think of anything more awful than being stuck on a boat in the middle of the sea for hours on end with people I find utterly boring.'

Including your husband, thought Horton. 'I take it gardening is more to your taste.' He indicated the magazines on the table and the plants crowding the conservatory. Uckfield's wife, Alison, was into flowers; he wondered if she knew Mrs Thurlow.

Her face brightened making her look at least five years younger. 'Yes. I specialise in fuchsias. Do you know they grow to a height of twenty feet in Brazil?'

'They always remind me of fairies,' Cantelli interjected. 'My wife likes them. We've got a couple of bushes in our garden but nothing like this.'

She positively beamed at him. 'Then I must let you have some cuttings, sergeant.' She shifted to the edge of her seat as if she was about to leap up and fetch them at that moment.

'Do you know if your husband went sailing with anyone last Friday?' Horton said.

The frown was back; she hovered over the chair. 'He didn't say. Someone at the yacht club might know: that's at Horsea Marina, where he keeps his boat. Now if . . .'

Time to be a bit more brutal. Her lack of concern was irritating him. 'Mrs Thurlow, earlier this morning the coastguards found your husband's boat in the Solent, but I'm sorry to say that your husband wasn't on board.'

If he thought he was going to shock her into some kind of reaction, concerned or otherwise, then he was quickly disappointed.

'Then where is he?' she said, matter-of-factly.

'That's what we're trying to find out.' He tried not to sound too cynical. 'Has he had any health problems lately?'

'Not that I'm aware of.'

'What about business or financial difficulties?'

'I don't know anything about the business. You'd have to ask at the office,' she answered impatiently. 'If you're thinking he could have deliberately thrown himself overboard then you're wrong.'

Why? He wondered. Time to turn up the heat. This would tell him how much she cared.

'There is something else that you should know, Mrs Thurlow. This morning a man fitting your husband's description was found on the beach at Portsmouth.'

'You mean dead?'

'Yes.' He held her gaze. Her surprise was genuine, but he saw no grief, even though she had immediately grasped his meaning.

'You think it's Roger and it's not an accident?'

'He wasn't carrying any identification and we would like to rule out the possibility that it might be your husband. Do you have something of your husband's that will help us to identify him, a comb or brush perhaps, for the purposes of DNA and a recent photograph?'

'But, if it's not an accident and Roger would never kill himself then you mean he was murdered. How was he killed?'

'It's too early to say yet, Mrs Thurlow.'

'You don't want me to identify him?'

She seemed remarkably calm about this, Horton thought. 'That won't be necessary. We'll be able to check from fingerprints and DNA.'

She scrutinised him as if trying to see inside his thoughts. He kept his expression neutral. Other women might have gone into shock, or had hysterics, but Mrs Thurlow simply nodded, lifted her chin, and squaring her shoulders set off with Bellman trailing her.

Horton rose, plucking at his shirt sticking to his back.

'Stiff upper lip type,' Cantelli muttered, pulling at his tie and undoing his top button. 'Either that or she's made of stone.'

'Take a quick look round the kitchen, Barney.'

Horton stepped outside to get a breath of air. It was almost as hot out as it had been in the conservatory. Here, as at the front of the house, the garden was beautifully tended and landscaped with curved borders and isolated flowerbeds bursting with fuchsias. Under a small clump of trees to his right was a teak garden table and chairs, while to his left a large greenhouse brimming with colour was situated.

There was no breeze and the sun was steadily climbing in a milky blue sky. In the distance, covered in a haze, he could see the gentle rising slopes of the South Downs and hear the soft rumble of traffic from the A27 three miles away to the south. Uckfield's house was further down on the edge of the village, a fairly new, small and select development of executive styled houses built about eight years ago. Try as he might Horton couldn't prevent his thoughts turning to his own house just outside Petersfield to the north of Portsmouth. He'd always hoped to return to it but he guessed that the letter burning a hole in his pocket would put paid to that.

Cantelli joined him. 'Last Friday has a ring around it on her calendar and the initials SWFS, otherwise nothing. There's a fuchsia society newsletter, some invoices from seed merchants, and the vet's telephone number pinned on her notice board and that's about it.'

Horton hadn't really expected Cantelli to find anything and certainly not a big circle around yesterday's date with the words 'kill husband!' Still it was always worth having a nose around to get the feel of a place. And this place, with the exception of the garden, said, 'tired'. He turned back to see Mrs Thurlow heading towards them.

'Will this do, Inspector?'

Horton took the comb and popped it into a plastic evidence bag. He saw her eyes flit to the large greenhouse on his right and she seemed eager to get rid of them. He wondered if they'd disturbed some kind of fuchsia potting out ritual.

He studied the photograph she'd also given him. It was of a tall, slender man in his fifties standing on the deck of a large motor cruiser. He was wearing navy shorts, a light-blue polo shirt and stained deck shoes. His silver hair was swept back off a suntanned, narrow face and he was smiling into the camera. In his hand was a champagne glass. The boat was in a marina, which to Horton's trained eye looked to be Cowes on the Isle of Wight. Who had taken the photograph? Not Mrs Thurlow by her own account, so a fellow crewmember, or a lover perhaps?

He handed the photograph to Cantelli who glanced at it before slipping it carefully into his notebook.

'What happens now, Inspector?' she asked, leading them to the front door.

'We'll let you know as soon as we have any news. Is there anyone you would like us to call? A friend or relative you might want.'

'No. Thank you. I'll be fine. I have Bellman.'

'There is just one more thing. Does your husband have any distinguishing features or scars?'

She shook her head. 'No.'

Horton handed over his card and urged her to get in touch if she heard from her husband, which he thought would be difficult unless she was clairvoyant. He was convinced that the body was Thurlow. He was also certain that Mrs Thurlow knew more than she was saying.

'She's a cool one,' Cantelli said, as he turned the car in the driveway. 'Which is more than can be said for that blessed conservatory and this car. She didn't even offer us a drink. I was nearly tempted to shove the dog over and slurp from his bowl.'

Yes, a nice cold glass of water would have been welcome, Horton thought as he called Uckfield.

'Get over to the mortuary,' Uckfield snapped after Horton had called to update him. 'And if Evans has regained consciousness you can pay him a visit too while you're at the hospital. There's a briefing at midday. Be here.'

Horton relayed the instructions to Cantelli then called the Marine Support Unit.

'The boat's as neat as nine pence,' Sergeant Elkins said to Horton's enquiry. 'There's been no fight or struggle. There's a sailing bag in one of the cabins.'

'Has it been unpacked?'

'No.'

'What about a tender? Is there one on board?'

'No, but there looks as though there should be.'

'Start the search for one, will you, Elkins? Check out the shores around the area and the marinas. Make sure nothing is touched and that Thurlow's boat is secure.'

'It's in the compound in the ferry port.'

As Horton rang off Cantelli said, 'You think she was lying about when she last saw her husband?'

'Could be. I don't think she much cared for him but that's no crime.'

'You reckon it's Thurlow then?'

Horton didn't hesitate. 'Yes.'

'And could she have killed him?'

Horton thought about the body laid out on the pebbled beach, the face smashed beyond recognition. Was it a random killing? Had the killer chosen the first person he met as his victim and killed instantly and spontaneously? Mutilation was common in such cases. But why was the body naked? A killer who killed randomly would hardly stop to undress the victim. Or had it been planned and the victim known to the killer? A crime of passion perhaps? Somehow he couldn't see Mrs Thurlow working herself up into a passion about anything except her fuchsias. Or was it a crime of hatred? Horton's fingers curled around the envelope in his pocket. Could he have done that to Colin Jarrett? Was hatred enough? It often was, but in his case certainly not enough to take someone's life.

He said, 'Why kill him on the beach? Why not closer to home or even on his boat? Why was he naked?' And why, Horton thought, lay him out like that? That was bugging him.

Cantelli said, 'She doesn't go on the boat.'

'She could be lying.'

'Doubt it, because that would mean leaving her precious fuchsias. I know what Charlotte's like about watering her garden, if we go away for more than one day in the summer she starts fretting about her tomatoes.'

Cantelli was right but it was early days yet and useless to hypothesize until they had an ID; the DNA and fingerprints on the comb might give them that. First though it was the mortuary. Hardly Horton's favourite place, but then whose was it, save the pathologist?

THREE

'Yes, a woman could have done it if she surprised him,' Doctor Gaye Clayton said in answer to Horton's question as he stared down at the body on the mortuary slab. The victim had been cleaned up but the battered face didn't look any better than when he'd seen it on the beach. He couldn't identify him from the photograph that Mrs Thurlow had supplied either. He would have defied the victim's own mother to identify him.

'How?' He stepped back and turned his gaze on the small, freckled woman in front him. To say Doctor Clayton had been a surprise was putting it mildly. He wasn't sure what he had expected but it wasn't someone who looked as if she'd just finished college.

She said, 'He could have been kneeling, she came up behind him and applied a Spanish windlass.'

'A what?' asked Cantelli, chewing his gum and studying the body with interest. Horton was always amazed that the mortuary smell never seemed to get to Cantelli.

'A piece of material is looped around the victim's neck and then tightened with a stick, like a tourniquet. If it's done quickly enough and the victim is a relatively weak person then it's possible.'

Cantelli said, 'Then she undressed him? Difficult undressing a dead body.'

'Yes, but not impossible.'

'Time of death?' asked Horton, trying to place Doctor Clayton's accent. West Country? He could hear Tom, the mortuary attendant, a big, brawny auburn haired man, clattering about in the background whistling a tune from *The Sound of Music.*

'There was rigor in the body and taking this into account, the air temperature and the rectal temperature I took at the scene I would say he had been dead about nine hours before he was found.'

'Which puts it at about nine o'clock last night.' Four days since Mrs Thurlow last saw her husband on Friday.

'Nine, ten, thereabouts,' Doctor Clayton confirmed. 'Not a very pleasant experience for whoever found him.'

'I did,' Horton bluntly announced. 'I was out running.'

'Oh.' She gave him a look that was both assessing and curious, which made him feel as if he was lying on the slab.

'Do you know if he was killed where I found him?'

'There is significant bruising and scratches on his back and legs. I think he was killed not far from where you found him, Inspector, then dragged up the beach most probably to prevent him from being covered by the incoming tide. He wasn't restrained. He was killed quickly. The photographer has taken some images of the marks on the body and I'll blow them up on the computer later and see what I can make of them. The forensic scientist, Jolliffe — is that his name — quiet man, all teeth and glasses?'

'That's him.' Cantelli smiled.

'He's taken samples for DNA checking and scraped off a layer of skin for the fingerprints.'

'Good, we can check that out almost immediately.'

Jolliffe would feed his information into the National Automated Fingerprint Identification System, which would come back with a result within minutes. DNA would take longer. The sooner they lifted Thurlow's prints from the comb the better.

'When can we have your full report, doctor?' Horton moved away, pulling off the green gown.

'If you leave me to get on with my work I'd say some time later today,' she answered brightly, then addressed the mortuary attendant. 'We can start now, Tom. The nice policemen are just leaving.'

Horton smiled. Outside the mortuary he said, 'You didn't tell me she was like that, Barney!'

Cantelli shrugged. 'What were you expecting?'

'I don't know, someone older, stouter, uglier and with a moustache.'

Cantelli laughed. 'She knows her stuff and she can hold her own. I've seen Uckfield try to brow beat her without the slightest effect and you know what he's like when he gets into his stride. A double decker bus couldn't stop him; if it ran over him he'd still sit up and give it a speeding fine.'

The corridor into the main part of the hospital smelt of cabbage and disinfectant but even that was better than the formaldehyde of the mortuary, Horton thought.

Cantelli continued. 'I suppose she's had to be assertive working in a still predominantly man's world, or so PC Kate Somerfield keeps telling me. I said she should try living in my house.' Cantelli dodged a woman pushing a grumbling elderly man in a wheelchair. 'I'm outnumbered save for Joe and he's not even five so hardly counts.

'I can see that Doctor Clayton has charmed you.'

'Well you've got to admit, she's a hell of a lot prettier than old Gorringe. God rest his soul.'

'Anyone's prettier than Gorringe, even you, Cantelli. What do you think now that you've seen the body?'

Cantelli looked thoughtful for a moment. 'It looks like Thurlow, same build, but I can't see Mrs Thurlow bashing his face in like that. Why wait until last night when she could have killed him on Friday night or over the weekend?'

Horton agreed but he didn't have any answers yet. 'Let's go and check how Brian is.'

Brian Evans was still unconscious. Horton had a quiet word with the constable while Cantelli spoke to Evans' wife, Maureen. It seemed the prognosis was good though, which was a relief.

Snatching a glance at his watch, Horton nodded at Cantelli, who said his farewells to Maureen and Horton did the same. Soon they were outside but they hadn't gone far when Horton saw, crossing the crowded hospital car park, a slight man, wearing a brightly patterned loose fitting shirt, over long navy shorts. He was limping. Horton could only see the back of him but there was no mistaking who he was.

His heart skipped a beat. At first he thought it was an illusion conjured up by his anxieties but no, walking steadily towards a blue Mercedes, was the owner of Alpha One and the man who had ruined his life: Colin Jarrett.

'Be back in a tick, Barney. Wait for me by the car.'

'Andy . . .'

But Horton was already half way across the car park.

'Not ill, are you, Mr Jarrett?' he said coolly, stalling him before he could climb into the car. He could see a blonde woman of about thirty-five sitting inside.

Jarrett spun round; his arm in a sling and a plaster across his bruised forehead. A range of expressions crossed his pinched face starting with shock, progressing to puzzlement and ending with anger. He looked as if he was about to explode. His neck muscles bunched and his bloodshot green-grey eyes narrowed with hatred. 'What the hell do you want?'

You, trussed up like a turkey and served up for dinner, Horton thought, staring at the sharp-featured man in his mid-forties. He had all the trappings of wealth: the clothes, the car, the blonde well-spoken wife, the boys at the Grammar School and a large house on Portsdown Hill, overlooking the city, but he couldn't disguise the fact that he'd come up the hard way, a boy from the streets of Portsmouth. His accent was too pronounced, his taste too ostentatious and his eyes too wary. 'Just enquiring after your health,' is what Horton actually said.

'Bollocks.'

'What happened to you? One of your customers get fed up with paying his exorbitant membership fee and give you a going over? I almost envy him.'

'What would you know about our fees?' Jarrett snarled. 'You wouldn't be able to afford a week's rate never mind a year. We're selective about who we let in to Alpha One.'

'So I've heard.'

'And what's that supposed to mean?'

'Whatever you want it to mean.' Horton shrugged as if he didn't much care anyway.

Jarrett fingered the large plaster. 'If you must know some little toe rag in a stolen Range Rover rammed me at the traffic lights at Horsea Marina, early hours of this morning.'

'Tch, tch, how very distressing for you.'

'Yes it was,' Jarrett snapped, his unshaven face flushing. 'And if you lot got your finger out and stopped harassing innocent men and started chasing some real criminals you might actually catch him.'

'Harassing? Who's harassing? Can't be me because, one, I'm not in the business of harassing and, two, you're not innocent.'

Jarrett let out a heavy sigh and rolled his tired eyes. 'Here we go again. You won't let up, will you?'

Horton stepped closer. 'No, I won't. Not until I find Lucy Richardson and get to the truth.' He could smell garlic on Jarrett's breath and the sweat from his unwashed body.

'Then you'll end up being chucked out of CID, pounding the beat; or picking up your dole money. Take your pick,' Jarrett quipped.

Horton wanted to ram his fist into Jarrett's face and wipe the mocking smirk from it. It took a supreme effort not to react. It was exactly what Jarrett wanted and if he couldn't pass this first test then he could indeed kiss goodbye to the job and any chance of finding out exactly what was going on at Alpha One.

'I run a perfectly legitimate business,' Jarrett continued. 'I've got nothing to hide and the sooner you get that into your thick skull the better. Lucy was just employed by me like any other girl. I have no idea why she decided to go squawking about you unless of course it was true and, like they say, there's no smoke without fire.'

Jarrett opened the car door but before he could step inside Horton grabbed hold of it preventing him. Jarrett flinched. It was a small victory but it would do for starters. Horton wanted to scare this man so shitless that he would have no option other than to come after him. When he did he'd be waiting.

'I'm a very patient man, Jarrett. I don't care how long it takes, but I will find out what is going on in Alpha One.'

'Then you'll have a bloody long wait.' Jarrett's eyes flashed with anger.

'For heaven's sake, Colin, get in,' the woman inside called out irritably.

Jarrett hesitated fractionally, then climbed in and slammed the door with a clunk. Horton stepped back as the Mercedes sped past him, already Jarrett had his mobile phone pressed to his ear with his free hand.

Horton grinned to himself as he made his way back to the car where Cantelli, jacketless and chewing gum, was waiting for him.

'Well?'

'Well what? I just enquired after his health.'

Cantelli climbed in the car and Horton followed suit. Cantelli turned to Horton with a troubled expression on his face. 'He's got powerful friends, Andy.'

He knew that. For a while he and Dennings, from the Vice Squad, had watched Alpha One from the vacant office opposite. They'd seen a prominent councillor enter it as well as one or two respected solicitors and well-known businessmen, and as far as he was aware there was nothing on any of them. He couldn't question them because they'd go squealing to Superintendent Reine, and they would warn Jarrett. It would also be the same with the staff. That left him with two courses of action: one to ride Jarrett as hard as he dared without getting kicked out of the police service, until he forced Jarrett's hand in some way, and the second was to find Lucy and get her to tell him the truth. But where was she?

On his return to work yesterday, he had checked criminal records. Nothing. She hadn't been picked up on any charges in the last two months since her disappearance. Then he had checked to see if she was claiming social security anywhere; she wasn't. So she had either been paid well to lie about him and was living off the proceeds, or she was holding down a job. If she was, then it was a black economy job because the Inland Revenue had no record of her paying any tax. His guess was that Lucy could afford not to work for some time but when the money ran out what then? She'd be back and he'd be waiting, ready. She'd show up again if only to ask for more money from the man who had paid her to lie. And he knew who that was despite all his protestations of innocence: Colin Jarrett.

'I can't leave it, Barney,' he said quietly.

'Revenge can be a cruel master.'

Horton shrugged. 'Then I'll take my chances.' He felt the letter in his pocket. His phone rang. It was Walters.

'The DCI is wondering if you're going to join him for the briefing, Inspector,' he said sarcastically. 'That is, if you're not too busy.'

'Course I'm busy. I'm trying to find out who the dead man is,' Horton snapped.

'Do you want me to tell the DCI that, guv?'

'No.' Horton guessed that Walters' interpretation of his remark would be something like tell the DCI to go screw himself. 'We'll be there in ten minutes.' He rang off.

As Cantelli threaded his way through the city streets Horton let his mind dwell on his chance encounter with Jarrett. There was something niggling him about it. He replayed it, hearing every nuance, seeing every glance and analysing every word. Maybe he was just clutching at straws, hoping he would read some hidden meaning into Jarrett's words or expression? For eight months he'd left the man alone despite wanting to beat the truth from him, knowing that if he did Jarrett would have won and he would have been kicked out of the police service quicker than you could say P45.

Day after day he had relived every moment of that operation. Night after night he had dreamt of it. He'd even gone so far as to make some notes but he'd ripped them up one night in a drunken rage.

His mind trawled back through the year. In March Catherine had thrown him out, she'd had enough of his drinking and his rage. In April, after he had continually pestered her, she had stopped him seeing Emma. In May and June he had got so drunk he could remember nothing, only in July had he come to his senses, when the case had been dropped. He'd been cleared on a technicality — Lucy had disappeared. That was about as much use to him as a hairpin in a hurricane. He had promised Steve Uckfield he wouldn't attempt to see Jarrett, or have anything to do with Alpha One. Steve had told him to move on with his life. He had intended to but now he knew how utterly impossible that was. He had always known despite his promises. Portsmouth was a big place, but not big enough for him to avoid Jarrett and vice versa. And his future was too irretrievably linked to his past to forget the man.

'Drop me at the marina, will you, Barney. I want to collect my bike. You return to the station; get those fingerprints over to the bureau for checking. If Uckfield asks for me tell him I'm on my way.'

FOUR

'What the devil did you think you were playing at?' Uckfield roared at Horton later that day.

I wasn't playing, thought Horton, standing ramrod stiff the other side of the DCI's desk. Who had told Uckfield about his encounter with Jarrett? Not Cantelli, surely?

'Jarrett's complained to the Super. Says you've been harassing him. Is it true?'

He might have guessed that Jarrett would go bellyaching right to the top. 'I spoke to him. I don't call that harassment.'

'Why didn't you ignore him, walk away?'

'Like you would have done?'

'Yes, if it meant keeping my job,' Uckfield quipped.

Horton cocked a sceptical eyebrow. After a moment Uckfield let out a sigh and threw himself back in his seat. Running a hand through his hair he said, 'The Super's just waiting for the opportunity to boot you as far away from here as possible, Andy, so why go looking for trouble? I covered up for you, said Jarrett must have misconstrued your words, but I can't keep doing it.'

Horton remained silent. He didn't like the way Uckfield had said that; he didn't need to be reminded that he owed Steve but it was as if he wanted to rub it in. Still he was right. The Super would probably declare a public holiday if he managed to rid the station of what he considered a rotten apple. Anyone who tarnished Reine's image, and subsequently the prospects of him climbing the greasy pole to the top, was about as welcome as a cold in the head. He'd have to tread a bit more carefully and slow down. All the same Jarrett had presented himself, he hadn't gone looking for him. That being so he wasn't about to look any gift horse in the mouth.

Uckfield leaned forward. 'I need you firing on all cylinders, Andy, not with half your mind on that tart Richardson and Alpha One. You know I'm up before the promotion board next Friday and there'll be a place on the new Major Crime Team for you if I get it. So let's get this case of our body on the beach solved quickly and find the little bastard that stabbed Evans. OK?'

'Yes, sir.' At least he wasn't being chucked off the case.

Uckfield waved him into the seat across his immaculately tidy desk. A large fan whirred gently in the corner behind the DCI but it did little to dispel the mid-afternoon heat, which hung over the room like an invisible cloak, suffocating and oppressive.

Uckfield said, 'So what did you get on Evans's stabbing from Westover?'

The youth had been reticent to the point of muteness. He had been accompanied by his father and the family solicitor who, between them, had made the boy sound so mild mannered that it made Clark Kent sound like Rambo.

'He says there were gate crashers at his party.'

'And you believe him?'

'Does the Pope believe in contraception?'

Uckfield gave the ghost of a smile. 'So where do we go now?'

'We continue interviewing the other kids, the ones we can find, and try and track down the ones we can't. The drug squad are helping with that. I've seconded Kate Somerfield to work with them.'

'Put Cantelli on it too.'

'I need him working with me, Steve, on the murder. DC Marsden can handle the stabbing investigation. He's quite capable.'

Horton saw Uckfield frown. Marsden was the fast track graduate and blue-eyed boy. 'It'll give him the chance to head up an investigation, under my guidance of course. See what he's made of.'

'I'm not having Evans' stabbing side-lined.'

'I'm not. I'm just utilising manpower,' Horton replied calmly.

Uckfield pursed his lips. 'I'm not sure . . .'

'Marsden's only waiting to go before the next promotion board. He'll be Chief Constable before any of us,' Horton said tauntingly. Uckfield flashed him a look, which said not before me sunshine.

'OK.' He stretched back in the chair and clasped his hands behind his head. 'Where are we with our beach body?'

Horton pulled off the tie he usually only wore to court but had donned in case Uckfield had called Superintendent Reine into his dressing down. He'd be cooler in a Turkish bath. 'Did you ask Alison if she knows Mrs Thurlow?'

'She's passed the time of day with her at various flower shows, says she's an expert on fuchsias; me I can't tell geraniums from gladioli. Have you spoken to anyone in Thurlow's office yet?'

Horton shook his head. 'No point until we confirm our victim is Thurlow.'

'What the hell are the fingerprint bureau doing? We should have had the fingerprint check ages ago.'

'Computer crash,' Horton fabricated.

'And where is that pathologist with her report. I thought you said we'd have it this afternoon. Typical bloody woman.'

Horton didn't like to say that Gorringe had been so slow that he made a slug look fast. 'Perhaps she got busy.'

Uckfield already had the telephone in his hand and was punching in the mortuary number. 'Anything more on those cars seen close to where the body was found?'

They'd had an early break, a man walking his dog had called into the mobile incident unit to report he'd seen four cars in the car park just after nine thirty: a blue Ford, a Toyota, a silver Mercedes and a Mini Cooper. He hadn't got their registration numbers; that would have made it too easy, Horton thought.

'It's early days yet. We've only just given the information to the local newspaper. They'll run it in tomorrow's edition but the radio station has been pushing it out since just after midday.'

'What do you mean she's left?' As Uckfield barked into the phone, there was a perfunctory knock on the door, and Cantelli poked his head round it.

'Doctor Clayton's here.'

'At last.' Uckfield slammed down the phone. I was beginning to think you'd forgotten us, doctor.'

'I'm hardly likely to forget you, Chief Inspector.' There was a glint in her green eyes as she threw herself into the chair beside Horton without waiting to be asked. Horton nodded at Cantelli to stay.

'I believe this is what you've been waiting for.' With a flourish she held out a buff coloured folder.

Uckfield took it and flicked it open. He gave it a cursory glance. 'OK, so tell me what you've found.'

She thrust her short fingers through her spiky auburn hair and said brightly, 'We're obviously still waiting for all the test results but I can confirm our victim died from asphyxiation and that he was beaten after death but not with a stone. A heavy club was used: a thick stick, something wooden anyway. I found fragments of splinters lodged in his brain and his eye sockets.'

Sitting there with her ankle resting over her knee and dressed in combats and a T-shirt, Horton thought she looked more like a PE teacher than a pathologist. And she sounded as if she was discussing a sports injury rather than a post mortem.

'He'd had a meal; I've sent his stomach contents for analysis, but it was only partially digested and hadn't moved to the small intestine. We're still looking at time of death between nine and ten last night. But that's not all . . .'

She paused and looked at each of them in turn. Horton saw Uckfield glance impatiently at his watch. He could tell Gaye Clayton had noticed it but she was not to be hurried. In that moment he knew what Cantelli had meant earlier about her not being browbeaten.

'He hadn't had sexual intercourse before he was killed, either straight or anally. But there is something that suggests he likes his sex a little spicier than maybe your average man,' she went on. Now she had all their attention. Horton looked at her eagerly and he saw Uckfield's interest quicken.

'I couldn't see them at first because they were hidden by the marks on his back and legs where he'd been dragged along on the stones, so I enhanced the images on the computer and took another look at the body. That's why I've taken so long to get back to you. I wanted to be sure. It seems your victim was into flagellation. Of course whoever killed him could have beaten him but the marks were not made directly before his death, and they were only on his buttocks.'

Cantelli whistled softly. 'Any idea what he would have been beaten with?'

'I would hazard a guess at a cane, or stick of some kind.' She jumped up. 'Now I must be going. I'm late already.'

No one asked for what.

'Do you think his wife went in for that kind of thing?' Uckfield posed when the door had closed behind Doctor Clayton.

Horton considered that as a possibility but only for a moment. 'Not if the victim is Roger Thurlow. I just can't see Melissa Thurlow into flagellation. Can you sergeant?'

Cantelli shook his head.

'He could have visited a brothel.' Horton suggested.

'Check with Vice. And you'd better run the MO through the Automated Crime Recording system, *if* the computers are working,' Uckfield added sarcastically. 'See if there's been a similar murder committed elsewhere in the country.'

'Already have done.' *What does he think I've been doing all day? Horton wondered.* 'There's nothing that matches the way our victim was laid out. Do you want me to talk to Doctor Lydeway at the University?'

'No. Psychologists are a waste of time.' Uckfield's phone rang and he snatched it up. 'About time . . . What? Then whose are they? Great!'

'No match on the fingerprints I take it?' Horton said, disappointed. It wasn't Thurlow. He'd wasted his time at Briarly House this morning. Roger Thurlow, despite his wife's denial, could either have thrown himself overboard or had an accident. Sooner or later his body would be washed up along the south coast.

'No. And whoever he is, no one loves him enough to have reported him missing. He's not on criminal records either, so back to square one.'

'We might get something from the DNA unit but that will take a couple of days. We'll follow up this caning lead until we get something more.'

'Yeah, and it had better be soon.'

'Pre-interview nerves,' Horton said to Cantelli, when they were out of Uckfield's hearing.

'The promotion board would do us all a favour if Uckfield got promoted. It would get him off our backs.'

Horton said nothing about Uckfield's promise to him that there might be a place for him on the Major Crime Team. It could be academic anyway although Horton was of the belief that Uckfield would get both the promotion to superintendent and the position.

'Telephone Mrs Thurlow and give her the good news.'

'From what we saw earlier I don't think she'll be that bothered.

'I'll see what Dennings has to say.'

Sergeant Tony Dennings' fifteen stone of muscle seemed to take up the small Vice Squad office on the second floor. He was alone and watching a portable TV and video. He punched the pause button on the remote control and greeted Horton.

'What can I do for you?'

Horton perched himself on the edge of the desk behind Dennings. 'Flagellation. Who's into it these days?'

'Anyone, given enough inducement.' Dennings rubbed his large fingers and thumb together.

'Anyone in particular specialise in it?'

Dennings gave the matter some thought. Horton watched his great round face take on a look of deep concentration. There was no hurrying Dennings. He should know because he'd spent some time with him watching Alpha One.

After a while Dennings said, 'There's a couple of places at Southsea, set back from the seafront, that could be worth a try. Why? Got a taste for it?'

Horton repressed a retort. Maybe Dennings just meant to be funny but it was a bit too close to the mark for him after all the accusations Lucy Richardson had hurled at him.

'It seems our victim went in for it,' he said evenly, but felt the tightness in his gut that the memories of Lucy and her accusations always aroused. 'I thought it might be worth calling on them to see if they recognise the description of the victim '

Dennings scoffed. 'The only thing they'd recognise, apart from his backside, is the colour of his money.'

'We've got little else to go on at the moment.'

'If I hear of anything, I'll let you know.'

And that was it. Horton hesitated. Dennings looked at him enquiringly. Time to ask some questions and take a chance on the consequences. If Dennings wanted to squeal to Uckfield or Superintendent Reine then so be it.

'Has there been any word on the street that Jarrett and his exclusive club aren't as squeaky clean as they appear to be.' Horton watched Dennings' reaction closely, but he gave nothing away only shook his great head slowly.

'Not a fucking dickie bird.'

'You are still looking, aren't you?' Horton raised his eyebrows.

'No. Strictly out of bounds.'

'Who says?'

'Our lord and master, Superintendent Reine.'

Reine was in charge of the Vice Squad. He hadn't backed Horton and neither had Superintendent Underwood, his boss in the Special Investigations Department. Both had believed Lucy. Why?

'What about Underwood?'

'Retired in May.'

Of course, Horton had forgotten, with all the turmoil in his life it was hardly surprising.

'Anyway we've got enough trouble out there without going looking for it.' Dennings jerked his head at the video where a woman in her thirties was bound and chained and in the process, it appeared, of having her nipple pierced, very much against her will. 'Picked that amateur video up from a house in Gosport. And there's more like it, worse in fact.'

'It's similar to what was found on Woodard, isn't it?'

Jonathan Woodard had been a company director of a thriving business retailing women's clothing. He'd been found with hundreds of pornographic images downloaded from the Internet as well as DVDs and videos depicting rape, mutilation and torture. Woodard had refused to reveal his sources but he had been a member of Alpha One. His arrest had led to Operation Extra.

'You're not following up the Alpha One connection?' Horton said incredulously.

'Why should we?'

'Well, where did the Gosport man get that stuff from?' Horton jerked his head in the direction of the video.

Dennings' answer was in his silence.

Horton shook his head with disbelief.

Dennings added, 'You know there was nothing to link Jarrett, or his business, with this.'

'Only because of me. Lucy put paid to that. The operation was compromised. But why did she wait three days before coming forward with that cock and bull story that I had raped her? She knew that by then there would be no

DNA evidence; it was her word against mine and we all know who was believed.'

'You know we have to tread carefully.'

'Oh yeah,' Horton replied sarcastically. 'Then why did she take off as soon as the operation was exposed? There has to be something going on, Tony.'

Dennings shrugged his massive shoulders and returned his attention to the video. 'If Jarrett's soiled we'll get him in the end.'

Horton could see he'd get nothing further from the big man but that didn't mean to say that Dennings didn't know anything. On the contrary, reading between the words, Horton guessed there was quite a bit that Dennings did know, and had been told not to say. Not for the first time Horton wondered whether Dennings was involved with Alpha One. Why hadn't Lucy Richardson picked on Dennings instead of him?

He had reached the door before Dennings said with a warning note to his voice, 'Leave Jarret alone, Andy.'

Horton held his eyes for a moment. He thought he saw genuine concern and maybe behind it a silent plea but his earlier suspicion was confirmed: Dennings certainly wasn't telling all he knew.

Horton called Marsden into his office and told him to get up to speed with Evans' stabbing. Marsden looked disappointed at being taken off the beach body case but pleased with being given the lead in his own investigation. Horton knew Walters wouldn't like it, being the senior in terms of years of service and age, but Walters would have to put up with it. He returned to the incident room and ran through the reports from the mobile incident unit and the teams out questioning the nearby residents. There was nothing that looked of immediate interest. Trueman would see that all the information was fed through the computer and cross-matched.

It was late by the time Horton climbed on his Harley. The fog wrapped itself around him like dirty cotton wool.

Instead of heading back to the boat though he diverted down Queens Street, towards the Historic Dockyard and the harbour entrance. Oyster Quays seemed as good a place as any to eat.

Parking and locking the Harley in the underground car park he surfaced into the Plaza and turned left towards the waterfront where most of the restaurants were, picking one out at random. It was fairly quiet being a Wednesday and the fog had deterred many except the die-hard partygoers and holidaymakers. Horton ate his pizza, drank his diet coke and paid his bill, then instead of returning to his bike, he struck out in the grey crepuscular world, until he came to the mall that housed Alpha One.

It looked innocuous enough but what went on behind those closed doors? He'd have given anything to find out. He looked up and wondered if the CCTV camera had picked him out. Who sat in there screening the men as they rang the bell and gave their names to be admitted only if they were on that elite list? He had come here for more than just a meal and a drink — whoever it was would recognise him and tell Jarrett he had been there.

He turned and made his way back to the bike. The fog closed in around him rolling off the sea and enveloping the seafront as he headed home. He could hardly see a thing in front of him. He tried to concentrate on the road ahead, squinting his eyes as though it would help him to see where he was going, but his head was full of Jarrett and Lucy and that letter from the solicitors. If he could prove his innocence would Catherine have him back? If he could just talk to her, reason with her.

He turned into Fort Cumberland Road and as he did there was a roar of an engine behind him. His eyes flicked to his mirrors but it was too late. He wasn't prepared. The car screeched past him with a squeal of rubber and cut him up. Instinctively he swerved and as he did he felt the wheels of the Harley slipping. Desperately he tried to bring the bike under control, his heart was hammering against his ribs. He was losing it. The bike slid along the ground and he was catapulted through the air as though ejected from a canon. Through his mind flashed pictures of Emma, a child mourning the loss of her father; then Catherine's smiling face.

He wrapped his arms around his head. The breath was sucked from him as he struck the hard ground. He was rolling over and over, down and down. His head was knocking against the tight fitting helmet like a cocktail shaker. The last thing he saw before he lost consciousness was the image of Jarrett's mocking face.

FIVE

Thursday

Horton punched in the security code and entered the ugly 1970s station. He could hear someone creating havoc in the cells. The air was blue with abuse and full of the pungent smell of disinfectant mixed with vomit and urine. He nodded at the custody clerk who looked as if he was on the verge of a nervous breakdown.

'Bad night?' Horton asked.

'Yeah, as bad as yours by the looks of things.'

Horton grimaced. 'You should see the other guy.'

When he'd examined his face in the mirror that morning it looked as though he'd been a couple of rounds with Mike Tyson. He had a bruise the size of a tennis ball on his forehead, one on his chin and he was sure his eye was going to close up by the end of the day. His neck was so stiff that he could hardly move it, which was why he'd taken the unprecedented step of taking a taxi into work. Normally, without the bike, he would have jogged but he didn't think his equally bruised and grazed legs would stand it.

When he'd regained consciousness he'd been lying on the shingle in about the only gap of beach that remained between the houses and the marina. It had been a miracle that he should land there. No one had come to his aid, probably because no one could see him in the fog. Slowly he had pulled himself up. Nothing had been broken thank goodness, but his head felt as though someone had been kicking it around a football field and his body as though it had been used as a punch bag in Colin Jarrett's gym.

For a while he had drifted in and out of consciousness. He'd had no idea of the time; lifting his arm to check his watch would have been a major operation and crawling along the beach to locate the Harley an expedition as challenging as climbing Mount Everest in the nude. But he had to move or get wet. Groaning and grunting he edged his way along the shingle until he stumbled on the Harley. He found his phone, which was still working, and called Malcolm Hargreaves who arrived fifteen minutes later, with his pick-up truck. After sucking in his teeth at the sight of the damage to the bike, and giving him a lecture on how to ride a Harley, he had finally admitted that it wasn't that bad: some scratches on the silver chassis, a couple of dents and a smashed headlamp.

Malcolm had offered to take him to casualty, but Horton had refused and eventually after a bit of arguing Malcolm dropped him at the marina with the promise that he'd have the bike 'good as new' by the following evening. Horton had eased himself down on his bunk after seeing to his battered body in the marina showers and then had slept so soundly that he hadn't woken until after nine and knew there was no point hurrying into work. He was late; another hour or so wouldn't make much difference.

He had called into the mobile incident unit before heading for the station but there was little to report. He made his way to his office trying to ignore his thumping head and the curious looks and raised eyebrows of his colleagues as he went. In the CID room Walters eyed him smugly.

'Chief's been asking for you, guv,' he said with relish, obviously scenting trouble.

'Then you'd better tell him I'm here,' Horton snapped, beckoning to Cantelli and fetching a plastic cup of water from the cooler. He closed the door with his foot. It wasn't a good idea. A pain shot up his leg causing him to groan.

'What happened? You look awful,' Cantelli said, clearly very concerned.

'A car cut me up in the fog. I came off my bike.' It was the truth. He didn't see why he should burden Cantelli with his problems when the man looked as though he'd been up all night. 'You don't look so hot yourself.'

'I'm all right,' Cantelli muttered uneasily, but Horton could see he wasn't. He wondered if the nephew he had helped keep out of prison was playing up again. Very little troubled Cantelli but his family were a different matter. 'Family all right, are they?' By Cantelli's reaction Horton saw that they obviously weren't. 'Sit down.'

Cantelli obeyed. Horton pushed open the window as far as it would go, but it only let in more stifling heat and the noise of the traffic. He closed the slatted blinds and switched on the fan. 'So what's up?'

'It's Ellen.'

She was the eldest of Cantelli's five children; quickly Horton calculated she must be about fifteen.

Cantelli said, 'She came home late on Tuesday night and very drunk. I laid into her a bit, you know out of relief, I guess. She had me and Charlotte almost out of our minds with worry. I grounded her for the rest of the week and the weekend and now she's not speaking to us.'

'She'll get over it.' Then Horton frowned. He could see there was more. 'And?'

'She lied about where she had been. Oh, she doesn't know I know that but I've checked. Sophie Mayhew told her mother she was on a sleep-over with Ellen at Jaz Cordiner's house. Sophie was out all night. Ellen was on no sleep-over, so where the blazes was she?'

'She came home though and she's OK, isn't she?' Horton asked, concerned. He didn't like to see Barney worried like this. He knew how he'd feel if it was Emma. He hoped to God he'd still be able to see Emma when she was fifteen and be there for her if she needed him. He rubbed his aching head as the thought conjured up Jarrett and the accident last night, which could so easily have been fatal. He could be mistaken about Jarrett being behind it but he didn't think he was. He hadn't seen the vehicle intent on despatching him to the other world but he had the impression of it being a dark saloon car with the registration letters PE. It wasn't much, and certainly not enough to run a vehicle check, but it was better than nothing.

He had hoped his visit to Alpha One would stir things up and it certainly had. He hadn't expected Jarrett to take action so quickly or be so violent. He was lucky to be alive. Jarrett intended to silence him, permanently if necessary. The thought should have worried him but it didn't. It cheered him. Now all he had to do was stay alive long enough to get evidence. He brought his attention back to his mournful sergeant.

'Sadie says Ellen's been crying a lot. They share a bedroom,' Cantelli explained. 'Charlotte tells me that it's fairly normal behaviour for teenage girls but it breaks my heart to think Ellen's unhappy. If someone's hurt her I'll kill them.'

'It'll be all right, Barney. She probably just needs a bit of time.' What else could he say?

Cantelli didn't look convinced.

'Let's get on with the case, shall we? Might keep both our minds off our personal problems.'

'Sorry. Yes, you're right.'

'So what's new?' Horton took a long draught of water, crushed the plastic cup with one hand and tossed it in the bin.

'We've managed to eliminate two of the cars seen in the car park. The owners of the Mini Cooper and the Toyota have both come forward. They seem pretty genuine. The Toyota owner is a married man having an affair with his secretary. He asked us to be discreet.'

Horton rolled his eyes. He wished he had a pound for every time he'd heard that.

'The Mini Cooper's owner is single but was with his girlfriend looking at the view.'

'What view? It was foggy.'

'I don't think that was the view he was talking about.'

Horton smiled, then winced as a sharp pain shot through his face and up to his head.

Cantelli continued. 'We've got nothing yet on the dark Ford and the silver Mercedes.'

Horton's phone rang. As he expected, it was Uckfield summoning him. He left Cantelli and headed down the corridor to the open door next to the CID main office.

Uckfield looked up, his anger swiftly changing to surprise. 'What happened to you?'

'Got knocked off my bike last night.'

'Are you fit enough to be at work?' Uckfield said, waving Horton into the seat across his desk.

With a wince Horton eased himself on to it. 'I'm alright.'

'Where did it happen? Did you see who it was? Have you talked to traffic?'

'No. I didn't see who it was. I was too busy trying to stop myself from being killed. It was just one of those things,' Horton said curtly. There was no way he was going to tell Uckfield about his visit to Alpha One or his suspicions that Jarrett had been driving that car. He saw Uckfield's scowl but quickly brought him up to date with their murder case. Uckfield listened, frowning, twirling his pen like a majorette's baton in his large fingers.

Horton added, 'Dennings has given me a couple of addresses where caning is a speciality. I'm putting some officers on to checking it but it's a bit slender.'

Uckfield puffed out his cheeks. 'This is just what I don't need now.'

Horton thought the opposite. In fact he was rather grateful to their murdered man. If it hadn't been for him he would never have bumped into Jarrett at the hospital and set in motion a chain of events that could have ended up with him being killed, but could just help him get to the truth quicker than he had anticipated. Sooner or later he had planned to return to Alpha One and confront Jarrett, and the dead man had just made him do it sooner.

Dismissed, Horton returned to his office. His head wasn't getting any better and it wasn't helped by the questions that kept swirling around it, which had little to do with the case and much to do with his past. He pushed some papers around his desk unable to concentrate and was just about to give up and check with the incident room when Cantelli poked his head round the door.

'A Ms Frances Greywell's just phoned. She's a partner at Framptons Solicitors; says her colleague Michael Culven didn't show up for work yesterday or this morning, and he should have done. He's in the middle of an industrial tribunal case. They've tried calling his home, and his mobile, but there's no response.'

'And?' Horton felt his pulse quicken. A thrill ran through him pricking the hairs on the back of his neck. Could this be the break they needed?

'He fits the description of our victim. Not only that, but he drives a silver Mercedes.'

Barely containing his excitement Horton plucked his sailing jacket from the back of his chair, his headache had suddenly improved. 'Where does he live?'

'Horsea Marina. Uniform are picking up Culven's cleaning lady now. She has a key.'

The patrol car was already outside Culven's modern three-storied house when they arrived and a skinny young woman was pacing up and down dragging heavily on a cigarette.

'About time,' she said, throwing the still smouldering stub into the gutter. 'I've left Darlene with a neighbour.'

'We won't keep you long Mrs—'

'Miss Filey,' she corrected Horton with a toss of her long dark hair and a glare of deep brown heavily made-up eyes. She sported three ear studs up each ear lobe and one on the side of her nose. The index finger of her right hand was stained yellow with nicotine and Horton could smell the cigarette smoke on her. She could have been any age between eighteen and thirty.

'What happened to you?' She sniffed. 'Got in a fight beating up some poor suspect, did you?'

'If you could just let us in.'

She scoffed before inserting the key in the lock and pushing back the door. She bent to retrieve the post from the mat, but Horton quickly restrained her, placing his hand on her bare arm. She looked at him with hostility before sighing pointedly and moving aside. Horton stepped in front of her and walked along the narrow passageway into the kitchen at the rear of the house. He then nodded at her to follow him, which she did with an elaborate flounce. As she stepped inside he pulled the door to behind her seeing Cantelli slip down and pick up the letters with latex-covered fingers.

Horton could tell instantly there was no one in the house, dead or alive. Death left a place much colder than this, you could smell it, taste it, and sense it. It crept up your flesh, quickened your breath, and sent your pulse racing to cope with the first shock of meeting it. But this house was empty, just a shell.

'How long have you cleaned for Mr Culven?' He moved to the wide patio doors, which opened onto a small courtyard garden and the marina beyond. It was stifling hot and his eyes quickly scanned the kitchen for a key to open the doors. There wasn't one visible. Culven's house, like many on this development, came complete with a berth but Culven's was empty and, from what Horton could see, there were no mooring lines lying on the ground. Culven could, of course, have taken the lines with him on his boat — if he had one — and if it hadn't conflicted with the fact that he'd hardly go sailing in the middle of one of his cases.

Miss Filey said, 'About a year. I come in twice a week. Mondays and Thursdays. Not that it needs much cleaning. He keeps it tidy like.'

Horton could see that. The lime oak kitchen with its shiny appliances looked as though it had come straight out of the showroom. 'Then you would have been here today.' It was a bit late for a cleaner he thought, one o'clock, but maybe she usually came in during the afternoons, or at any time to suit her.

She looked at him suspiciously. 'Yeah, I was just on my way here when you lot showed up at my flat. Nosy bugger neighbours will think I've been nicked.'

'We saved you the bus fare then. Did you see Mr Culven on Monday?'

'No.'

'So when was the last time you saw him?' Horton added, when clearly she wasn't going to be forthcoming.

'As it happens I never sees him. Well, hardly ever. He's gone to work when I come in.'

'How does he pay you?'

'He leaves me money on the breakfast top there, don't he? Not that it's worth the bother. Tight fisted old git, minimum wage like it or lump it. Typical lawyer always telling you they're hard up and then charges you a fortune if you so much as fart in their presence.'

Horton couldn't have put it better himself but her words served to remind him that soon he'd have to consult a lawyer. 'When does he pay you?'

'Every Thursday like.' He saw her looking round. 'And it's not here. Well if he thinks I'm going to clean for nothing then he can think again.'

'Miss Filey,' Horton called out sternly, as she was about to march out.

She stopped, sighed and turned round. 'Now what?'

'Was your money here last Thursday?'

'Yeah, why shouldn't it be? Look what's this all about? He done a bunk with some old bag's money?'

'When did you last see Mr Culven?' he asked wearily.

'I dunno, must be about three weeks ago. He had a morning off or something.'

'Is he married?'

'What him?'

'What do mean?'

'You obviously haven't met him. If you ask me, he's one of them, you know what I mean.' She raised her eyebrows.

'A homosexual?'

'Yeah. Not that I've got anything against them, mind. Not if they keeps themselves to themselves but they don't, do they? They have to keep on ramming it down your throat like.'

Cantelli, returning from his quick initial inspection upstairs, overheard the last remark, spluttered and quickly turned it into a cough. She looked at him as if he'd grown two heads. 'What's up with him?'

'He's not been well. Have you ever seen any evidence of a man living or staying here, Miss Filey?'

'No, can't say I have. But a man what lives alone, and don't have no female friends, well he's got to be a bit weird, hasn't he?'

She'd just described him! Maybe like him Culven didn't live alone by choice. Perhaps somewhere there was an ex Mrs Culven.

'I've got to get back. Here's the key.' She thrust it at him. 'You can bring it back for me for Monday, *if* I've still got a job to come to and you buggers haven't banged him up.'

She didn't seem to care if they had, Horton thought. She flounced out, the cheeks of her neat backside showing just beneath her tight shorts. The door slammed behind her. The patrol car would drop her back home.

'Right little madam, that one,' Cantelli said.

Horton pulled on his latex gloves. 'Find anything upstairs?'

'Nothing of any interest.'

Horton opened the fridge. It was well stocked so Culven had had no intention of disappearing. Horton sniffed at the contents but nothing seemed to have gone off so he couldn't have been gone long. There was also bread in the wooden bread bin, which wasn't mouldy, and plenty of tins in the cupboards.

Cantelli said, 'There's some dirty washing in the linen basket in the bathroom, usual medicines in the cabinet; looks like he suffers from migraine and indigestion.'

'And he likes microwave dinners.' Horton pushed his foot on the pedal bin and peered inside. 'Check the garage. That looks like the key on the hook over there.'

Cantelli lifted it from the corner cupboard and disappeared into the hall. Horton had found the key to the patio doors in one of the drawers and stepped out into the courtyard. A hot humid breeze did nothing to cool the temperature but instead seemed to suck in all the air. The sky was like a field of pale blue flax. The sun glinted off the sea so that it sparkled like a million pieces of shattered glass. He hoped to God that this time they'd found their victim and that this wasn't going to be one of those frustrating cases where nothing ever seemed to come together. The first few days in an investigation were vital and if they couldn't even identify their victim then they wouldn't be able to begin to understand the profile of their killer or the motive.

Cantelli returned with a shake of his head. 'No car, just usual stuff: some tools, a sun lounger, a couple of old chairs and packing cases. I couldn't see anything inside them but I didn't like to touch too much in case Culven's our victim.'

Horton stepped back inside and followed Cantelli up the stairs to the middle floor. A swift tour showed him a lounge with a balcony overlooking the marina, a small dining room, a room that Culven clearly used as a study, and a toilet and shower room. There were no pictures on the magnolia-painted walls and no mirrors. Clearly Culven was not interested in his environment, neither was he vain.

'Looks as though he's just moved in,' Cantelli said.

'He's been here a year at least, according to the delectable Miss Filey.'

'Not the homely sort then.'

But I am, or rather I was, Horton thought with bitterness. Living with Catherine and Emma had been the first real home he'd had. After being raised in children's homes and then shoved from foster parent to foster parent he thought he had found utopia.

He pushed open the glass doors and stepped out onto the balcony, trying to push away unhappy memories. Here he had a better view of the boats in the marina. They were spread out in neat rows behind their pontoons and in the near distance were the lock gates to the marina. On the other side of the marina there were more houses and apartments. To his left was the boardwalk and beyond that towards the lock, the chandlery and yacht club.

Cantelli said, 'Didn't Mrs Thurlow say her husband's boat is kept here?'

'Yes and Uckfield's.' He broke off as his eyes alighted on a man walking down one of the pontoons. He couldn't mistake that figure or that face, now minus its sticking plaster. He watched Jarrett climb aboard a large motor cruiser and disappear from sight. It appeared he was alone.

'Let's take a look around.' He turned abruptly hoping Cantelli hadn't seen Jarrett. The warning from Uckfield wasn't going to put him off confronting Jarrett but he didn't want to involve Cantelli, or put him in a position where he might have to lie to cover up for him. The sergeant had enough on his plate.

Cantelli began poking about the videos and DVDs in a bookcase. Horton scanned the room with its faded furniture, which looked as though it had come as a job lot from a second-hand shop. The pale blue Dralon sofa had threads hanging loose from it. A single chair of the same material was placed at an angle in front of the television and, judging by its state, was the one that Culven favoured of a night as he sat eating his TV dinners. Horton got the impression of a sad, lonely man who'd either given up on life, or who was too mean to refurnish his new home.

He crossed to the bookcase to the left of the fireplace. 'Interesting reading matter,' he said, craning his neck at the various titles haphazardly placed: Robert Jordan and Terry Brooks, *Witch War* by James Clemens, and Stephen King. 'Fantasy and horror.'

'His videos and DVDs look the same. He's awfully keen on Emma Peel by the looks of it. Man's gone up in my estimation.'

'Doesn't play much music.' There were only a handful of CDs, mainly country and western. Some Horton liked and had in his own collection, which was still in his house. He wondered what Catherine had done with them? Probably packaged them up and stuck them in the garage knowing her, out of sight out of mind, which seems to be what she had done with him. 'I'll take a look in his study,' he said.

It was a poky room that could barely take the large old pedestal desk pushed up against the wall and which clashed with the style of the house. He wondered if Culven had downsized from a larger family home bringing with him some heirlooms, or perhaps his ex-wife hadn't wanted these things?

He stood at the window to the right of the desk. He saw that Jarrett had removed the canvas cover from his motor cruiser, an expensive sleek Sunseeker Portofino 46. Did that mean he was going out for the day or just sun bathing on board? Neither was a crime. He could tackle him about the accident but Jarrett would only deny it.

He turned away and sat in the old leather swivel chair pulling open the desk drawers. Everything seemed to have been shoved in any old how. He picked up an address book and flicked through it, the usual: doctor, a couple of other names, perhaps relatives or friends, and his dentist. Underneath the address book were some bank statements. Horton made to pull them out when Cantelli called him.

'What is it?'

Horton found Cantelli in the lounge sitting on his haunches in front of a display cabinet that had little in it to display except some tired looking ornaments and a few dusty glasses; obviously Miss Filey's cleaning didn't extend this far. The cupboard doors at its base were open.

'Take a look at these.' Cantelli handed across two photographs he'd extracted from envelopes.

Horton could see by Cantelli's expression that he was excited about his discovery. Horton stared at the man in the photographs feeling his own pulse beginning to race. He was tall, lean, with wispy, grey thinning hair and a rather bemused expression on his narrow face as though the person taking the picture had startled him. He was standing by a silver Mercedes. That had been one of the cars seen in the car park. The other photograph was of the same man on a small motorboat. It was a Sealine 25.

Horton looked across at Cantelli. 'Our victim? Or our killer?'

'That's not all.' Cantelli pulled himself up, smiling broadly. In his hand was a bundle of letters held together by a large paperclip. 'We might also have found our motive.'

Horton looked at him speculatively.

'They're from Melissa Thurlow and they're not about growing fuchsias.'

SIX

Culven's fingerprints matched those of their body on the beach. The forensic team went into Culven's house and officers were deployed to question the neighbours. Now they knew who the victim was the investigation could step up a gear. Uckfield was happy. He thought they might also have a suspect: Roger Thurlow.

Horton wasn't so sure. 'If he killed Culven then why not use his boat to make his escape? Why abandon it like that?'

'As a decoy to throw us off the scent,' Uckfield said. 'He certainly had the motive to kill Culven. He could have used his tender to take the body onto the beach and then drag Culven along the stones out of the tide's reach.'

But that didn't tie up. 'Both Doctor Clayton and the head of the scene-of-crime team, Phil Taylor, say that Culven was killed on the beach. Thurlow would hardly have needed to put him in his tender.'

'Perhaps Thurlow arranged to meet Culven on the beach, killed him and had his tender already there to make a quick getaway after killing Culven.'

'OK. We'll talk to the Harbour Master and the Harbour Conservancy; they have regular night-time patrols who might have seen or heard something. But if Thurlow did kill Culven, and then ditched his boat, he could be out of the country by now.' Or dead, Horton thought, reverting to his original theory. Thurlow could still have had an accident. Or maybe he had never made it back to the *Free Spirit* after killing Culven, which was more likely: navigating a small tender in the dark and fog would have been nigh on impossible even with hand-held GPS.

Cantelli had been despatched to Melissa Thurlow to confront her about the letters and obtain a sample of her handwriting. Horton had sent a WPC with him. He didn't think that Melissa Thurlow would need comforting when she learned her lover was dead but two sets of eyes were better than one when it came to observing and gauging reaction. Meanwhile he decided to test out his aching legs and walk the half-mile to Frampton's Solicitors along the busy London Road, which led out of the city. He was quickly ushered into the managing partner's spacious office.

'It isn't like Michael not to show up for work without warning, especially in the middle of a case,' Frances Greywell said, waving him into a seat across her wide desk. Her oval face was serious beneath the short, sleek, bobbed hair and her dark eyes searched his for his reaction. When he gave none she continued, 'When he didn't show for work yesterday we thought he might be ill. He wasn't answering his phone. Then when I read about the body being found on the beach in last night's paper and that you were trying to trace the owner of a silver Mercedes, I spoke to the other partners this morning and we agreed to contact you.'

'So Tuesday was the last time you saw Mr Culven?'

'Yes. He left the office that evening just before me at seven o'clock.' She sat forward in the beige leather chair looking concerned. 'Can you tell me? Is the body on the beach Michael's?'

'Yes. But I'd appreciate it if you didn't say anything yet. We need to inform his relatives. I thought you might know who he named as next of kin.'

It was as if she hadn't heard him. 'Who could have done such a terrible thing? And to Michael? I can't believe it, Inspector.'

'I'm sorry.'

She pushed a hand through her chestnut hair which swung back exactly into place just like Emma's he thought.

Frances Greywell said, 'It was murder?'

Horton nodded.

She let out a sigh and remained silent for a moment. Then visibly pulling herself together said crisply, 'Sorry, you wanted to know next of kin.' She picked up her telephone and punched in a number. 'Amanda, bring me Michael's personnel file please.'

Horton admired her efficiency. He expected it. Both her appearance and her office said crisp, professional, focused.

'What did Mr Culven do here?' he asked, wondering for a moment whether Ms Greywell and her firm would be a match for Catherine's solicitors *if* he decided to consult them. For the present he hadn't even opened that blasted letter.

'He is . . . was our company commercial partner specialising in corporate matters: employment law, management takeovers, mergers and acquisitions that kind of thing. He was clever, a very good lawyer.'

'What about his private life? Friends, hobbies, interests?' Did she know that her fellow partner had been having an affair and that he liked being caned? He doubted it. Why should she?

Frances Greywell pressed her well-manicured hands together to form a triangle as she considered his question. He could see she wore no wedding or engagement ring.

'He was a quiet man, not one for small talk but he did enjoy going out on his boat. It was one of the reasons he moved to Horsea Marina, after his mother died, so that he could have his own berth.'

'Was he married or has he ever been married?'

'Not as far as I'm aware. He once told me that he liked his freedom and independence.'

'Would you say he was attractive to women?'

'I'm sure some women would find him attractive but he wasn't my type.'

She smiled and Horton got the impression that she wanted him to ask her what her type was. He sidestepped that one.

'Has he ever been tempted? Anyone special, at any time?'

'I don't think so.'

The door opened after a perfunctory knock and a small, dark-haired woman in her late twenties entered carrying a file. She smiled rather nervously at Horton but he could see the curiosity and excitement shining in her eyes. Even if Frances Greywell said nothing, he knew the news would spread around the firm like a bush fire by tomorrow morning, probably had already.

Frances Greywell thanked her. After consulting the file she said, 'Michael has a sister, Maureen Brinkwell, she lives in New Zealand.' She handed a form across to Horton who quickly flicked down the details. Culven was fifty-three, born 8 September, a bachelor and non-smoker who had joined the firm's personal health care plan five years ago. Wouldn't do him much good now, Horton thought.

'Could I have a copy?' he asked.

'Of course.' She made to rise but Horton forestalled her.

'Could I also see Mr Culven's diary?'

'I'll call it up for you. Everyone's diary is on our computer system,' she explained, punching something into her keyboard. 'If you'd like to . . .'

He rose and moved around the desk to stand next to her. He could smell her soft perfume: light enough to state her femininity without compromising her professionalism.

'Just scroll up or down if you need to see more,' she said, swivelling her face to look up at him. She was very close. She held her position for a moment before straightening up. 'I'll get this copied for you.'

As he sat in her chair he wondered what element of law she specialised in. There was nothing on her desk to give him any clue. What if it were matrimonial? How would he feel telling her about Lucy Richardson? The answer was in the involuntary tensing of his body.

He quickly moved the cursor over the diary. There was nothing of interest in it for this week, except the industrial tribunal case, so he went back, an entry caught his eye. Yes! Culven had had a lunchtime appointment with Roger Thurlow at the yacht club at Horsea Marina on Friday, the last day that Thurlow had been seen. He went back further through July and June. There were several appointments with Thurlow, but what also interested him was the number of appointments with Jarrett. Before he had time to digest this the door opened.

Frances Greywell handed him the photostat copy, which he folded and placed in the pocket of his jacket.

'Was Mr Culven, Roger Thurlow's solicitor?'

'Yes.' She tried to hide her surprise and curiosity at the connection.

'And Colin Jarrett's?'

She nodded, now even more perplexed. 'I believe Michael's done . . . did a lot of work for Mr Jarrett. His business interests have expanded rapidly over the last five years.'

Tell me about it! Hotels, restaurants, gyms and health clubs all along the south coast. He could see that she wanted to ask him why he wanted to know. Before she could he said, 'I'd like a copy of this diary?'

'Of course.' Once again the lawyer, she said crisply, 'Which months do you want, Inspector?'

'June onwards.'

She moved back into her own seat brushing against him as she went. He thought it was intentional but maybe he was just kidding himself. She was attractive, but he was off women, except for one and she wanted nothing to do with him.

'The printer is in Amanda's office.'

He followed her through, admiring her slender but shapely figure. She had a way of walking, of doing things that said I know who I am, I know what I'm doing and I know what I want.

He said, 'Mr Culven had an appointment at Thurlow's on Friday lunchtime. Any idea what that was about?' He could see that she wanted to ask him about this obsession with Thurlow. She didn't though, probably because she knew he would only blank her out.

She said, 'Janet might know, Michael's secretary, but she only works part time. I'm afraid you've missed her. I can find out for you.'

'Please. I'd also like the paperwork of all the cases that Mr Culven had been working on, say, in the last six months.' That should give him an insight into Jarrett's business affairs. Not that he expected to find anything brazenly illegal but he hadn't spent three years in Special Investigations without knowing how to read between the lines. A glow of satisfaction spread through him. It had been a good move coming here instead of going to Melissa Thurlow's.

'The cases are confidential, Inspector.'

'I can return with a warrant.'

'Then you had better do so.' She handed him the print-out of diary dates. After a moment she said rather anxiously, 'Do you think Michael's death could be work-related?'

'It's too early to say.'

'Of course.' She gave a small frown of irritation at his stock answer.

'Could you lock his office and touch nothing. I'll send a couple of officers along tomorrow, with a warrant to search and seize anything that might have relevance to the case.'

'When can I announce it to the staff?'

'We'll let you know as soon as we've spoken to his next of kin.'

The heat was intense as he struck out for the station, but he hardly noticed it. He felt buoyed up with optimism. His fingers itched to get hold of Culven's files in relation to the work he had done for Jarrett. He wished he could start now. It was irritating that she hadn't let him see them but then he should have expected her to ask for a warrant, being a solicitor. Still, he could have one by tomorrow.

He turned his mind to the case. By both Frances Greywell's and Miss Filey's accounts of Michael Culven, and judging from what he'd seen of his house, he seemed a very ordinary man, fairly innocuous, certainly not the type to get himself brutally murdered like that. But then there was evidence that he liked being caned and if the letters from Melissa Thurlow were anything to go by he had been a passionate and energetic lover. So perhaps there was a lot more to Michael Culven than met the eye. And the evidence of those letters and Thurlow's disappearance suggested this was a crime of passion, a jealous husband outraged at his wife's infidelity.

Cantelli wasn't back but Marsden was and waiting for him. Horton could see immediately that he'd made a breakthrough on Evans' stabbing. His body was bursting with excitement. Horton knew the feeling. He'd missed that over the last eight months. Soon though he would experience it again, and he didn't just mean nabbing Evans' attacker, or even Culven's killer though both would be enough to send the adrenaline rushing through his body.

'I think I've tracked down the gate crasher, sir,' Marsden said, eagerly. 'The drug squad got hold of some names and I've been checking them out. Stevie Mason fits the description given by those kids who can remember being at the party. I'm just going round to ask John Westover if he knows him, or can recall seeing him.'

'What's Mason's form?'

'Arrested and fined for drug dealing five years ago outside the Sir Wilberforce Cutler Comprehensive School. Served two years for assault in a young offenders' institution, released a year ago. Prior to that, in and out of trouble since the age of nine.'

'OK, let's go bring him in.'

Marsden looked surprised. 'I thought I'd see what Westover has to say first.'

'And give Mason time to do a bunk?'

Marsden's fair good-looking face flushed. 'I don't think I've got enough on him yet.'

'And by the time you've got it the whole of the drug network will be buzzing with the news and Mason will have blown. Probably has already.'

'No, he's still in his flat off Queen Street. Somerfield is watching it.'

Horton glanced at his watch. 'Come on then. We'll take a couple of uniformed lads with us. I've got a feeling Mason won't come quietly.'

He didn't. With the sixth sense of the criminal fraternity Mason seemed to smell them coming from about six hundred yards away, certainly by the time they stepped out of the lift into the echoing corridor. But on the nineteenth floor of the tower block there was no way out of the flat except through the front door. The lifts and stairs, including the emergency stairs, were blocked by Horton, Marsden and two very large police officers.

Mason, a skinny young man in his early twenties, with bad skin and broken teeth, eyed them with alarm, dashed a panicky glance over his shoulder, saw there was nothing for it but to plunge ahead and came charging at them with a great bellow and a flash of steel in his left hand. But Horton was prepared for it. Sidestepping, he grabbed him roughly, swiftly disarmed him, threw him to the floor, pinned his arms behind him and rubbed his face in the ground.

'He's all yours, Marsden,' he said, leaving the two officers to take over the restraint and Marsden to charge him. He entered the youth's flat. It was filthy. It smelt of dirt, tobacco smoke, sweat and urine and he made sure to be careful where he trod. Discarded takeaway trays littered the two-bedroom hovel along with heaps of clothing, newspapers and cigarette ends. There were pornographic magazines on the bed, along with some items of girls' clothing and numerous beer and lager cans.

He crossed to the television and switched it off feeling a sense of sadness. Such a waste. Mason, he guessed, was beyond helping; perhaps he didn't have the brains, or perhaps he'd never been given a chance like he had. Horton's last foster parents had been the saving of him, the only couple who had recognised a young frightened boy, whose frustration at not being understood had found an outlet in violence.

But even then, as Horton surveyed this despicable room, he knew his violence had never spilled over onto others, only inanimate objects and sometimes himself. He had also been the opposite of this; obsessively tidy and clean, controlling his environment and, as he grew older, controlling his body through physical exercise, fearful that if he let go, if he showed he cared, he'd be punished or hurt.

He'd come a long way since then and had finally learned to love, only to have that denied him. His body went rigid. He told himself that he was strong, that he needed no one. It helped a little, but inside him he knew it wasn't true and never would be.

'You all right, sir?' Marsden's voice broke through his thoughts.

He spun round. Yes, he was all right. He had to be. What other choice was there? 'Let's get back and see what the little scum bag has to say for himself.'

SEVEN

Two hours later Horton and Cantelli were sitting in the corner of a dingy pub near the police station where Horton was washing the taste of Stevie Mason from his throat with a large diet coke and Cantelli was thawing out with a non-alcoholic lager after a spell in Mrs Thurlow's greenhouse.

'I felt like Humphrey Bogart in *The Big Sleep,'* Cantelli said. 'My shirt's only just drying out.'

'Mrs Thurlow didn't try and sit in your lap while you were standing?' Horton said, recalling one of the most famous lines from the film.

Cantelli grinned. 'No, and I didn't come across Lauren Bacall either, more's the pity. When I told Melissa that the dead man was Michael Culven she looked surprised but not upset. She knew he was her husband's solicitor and that's about it, or so she says.'

'You believe her?'

Cantelli sipped his drink as he thought for a moment. 'I don't know. She strenuously denies any affair and when I said her husband could have killed Culven in a jealous rage I thought she was going to burst a blood vessel laughing. Yeah, the ice lady melted. She insists that she hardly knew Culven, had only met him a couple of times. She appeared to be telling the truth, but how could she be with those letters?'

In front of them were copies of Melissa Thurlow's handwriting and the letters she had written to Michael Culven. Horton gazed at them. To him the handwriting was identical but he was no expert. It was being checked out by those who were. They already knew there were only Culven's fingerprints on the love letters. But what about in Culven's house?

They could lift Mrs Thurlow's fingerprints from the photograph of her husband that she'd given them earlier but her prints might not be the only ones on it, discounting Horton's and Cantelli's, so tomorrow an officer would go out to Briarly House to take her fingerprints and then they'd see if they matched any in Culven's house. It was too early to say how many sets of prints there were in Culven's house but Horton didn't envy the officer taking Miss Filey prints.

Cantelli said, 'She claims they're forgeries.'

'Then they're damn good ones.'

'I challenged her about not being concerned over her husband's disappearance. She said that sitting inside the house weeping and wailing was not her style.'

Horton could believe that. 'Where was she on Tuesday night?'

'At home, alone, except for the dog.'

'Pity he can't talk then.'

'And there's something else . . .'

Horton waited.

'She didn't answer the door so I walked around the side of the house, past the garage. Inside was a dark blue Ford.'

The same make and colour of a car seen in the car park the night Culven was killed.

Cantelli said, 'I made a note of the registration number.'

The door opened and Uckfield scanned the dim interior. Spotting them he made a cupped gesture with his right hand, Horton nodded, Cantelli shook his head and rose.

'I'll leave you to brief the DCI. I'd like to get home, unless there's anything else.'

'No. Give my love to Charlotte, and Barney . . . good luck with Ellen.'

Uckfield put a pint of diet coke and half a bitter on the small round table. 'The letters?' he asked, after taking a long draught of the local brew.

Horton pushed them over and studied one of them again as he considered Cantelli's feedback.

I can't give up my home and garden and I don't want to, darling. If I can only get Roger to agree to leave. I'm working on it but he has become so unpredictable that I am growing concerned. Oh not about me but for him.

Roger is drinking too much. I've begged him to see a doctor but of course he won't. When he's drunk he is more violent than ever and, darling, I am getting really worried. He's threatening all sorts of things against you. I don't think he'll actually do anything, you know Roger, all talk, but we must be careful. I've told him our affair is over. It's the only way to stop him. Be patient my love. We'll do as we agreed, we must stick to that no matter what.

Horton looked up leaving Uckfield to flick through the rest of the letters. A couple of middle-aged men in ill-fitting suits lingered over their drinks, their backsides spread over the narrow stools, the seats of their trousers shiny with wear. An old man peered at him from the far corner through rheumy eyes and a gnome like woman with frizzled grey hair and hunched shoulders, sucked on a cigarette, like a baby sucking on its bottle, as she avariciously fed coins into a games machine that had been rigged rarely to pay out.

Political correctness and good taste had by-passed this pub; it stank of cigarette smoke and chip fat. There was a large blackboard in the far right hand corner of the bar that advertised Karaoke and curry night on Thursdays. It was the nearest pub to the station, and its style and age were in sharp contrast to the newly built hotel and high technology business centre, with its units to rent by the hour and day. It served one of the poorest parts of Portsmouth, the mean little terraced houses and high rise flats. Horton knew the area well. He'd lived here once with his mother before she had abandoned him.

Uckfield sat back. 'What does she say?'

Horton relayed Cantelli's conversation with her but as he did he saw Uckfield's attention wander to two girls entering the bar. Horton frowned following his gaze. The girls were in their early twenties, one bottle blonde with lank hair, a pasty complexion and skinny white legs underneath a tight micro skirt, the other dark, with rolls of fat and a tattoo showing between the gap in her tight Lycra trousers and skimpy T-shirt.

'I'll take the blonde one,' Uckfield said, as the girls glanced over at them. Horton saw them giggle. He scowled. 'Just joking,' Uckfield said. 'You used to have a sense of humour.'

'I used to have a lot of things,' Horton quipped. Then added quickly before Uckfield could comment further, 'Cantelli saw a dark blue Ford in Melissa Thurlow's garage.'

'A clandestine meeting between her and Culven?'

Uckfield's eyes once again swivelled to the girls and it made Horton wonder if Uckfield ever played away from home? If he did then he was a fool and didn't know when he was well off. He recalled an almost forgotten conversation he'd had with Steve the night he had first met Alison Uckfield. 'I'm going to pull her and secure my chances of promotion into the bargain.' Uckfield had joked. A year later he had married the Chief Constable's daughter.

Horton said a little stiffly, 'Why meet her lover and then kill him? That doesn't make any sense. Anyway there are hundreds of dark blue Fords about. It might have no bearing on the case at all.'

Uckfield nodded at Walters and a couple of other officers who had just entered the pub. 'I didn't say, good work on Evans' stabbing.'

'Marsden deserves the credit for that. I told you he was bright.'

'I hear Mason came at you with a knife and you disarmed him.'

Horton shrugged. 'All in the line of duty as they say. Mason wasn't very forthcoming at first but Somerfield managed to get Westover to talk. When he knew we had Mason in custody he confessed to knowing him and buying ecstasy from him for the party. He didn't expect Mason to show up there but when he did he couldn't chuck him out. Westover's parents are having a blue fit.'

Uckfield sighed. 'Yeah, it's hard to believe what your kids are up to sometimes. I'd skin my two girls alive if I found out they'd been mixing with the likes of Stevie Mason.'

Horton would too if it happened to Emma, but he knew how easy it was for them to succumb to peer pressure. How did you stop them, short of locking them up? He couldn't help thinking of Cantelli and his daughter Ellen. Uckfield's eyes wandered again to the girls who were very conscious of his glances.

Horton said, 'Once Mason knew that Westover had grassed on him he admitted the drugs but said he didn't stab Evans.'

'And you believe him?'

'Do I believe in alien life forms?'

'Only if they come in the shape and form of toe rags like Mason.'

Horton smiled. 'He did it all right; we just have to get enough evidence now to prove it. I think we will. Somerfield and Marsden are continuing to work on witness statements.'

'One down, another one to go. Be nice if we could clear up Culven's murder before my promotion panel, do us both a bit of good.'

Horton silently agreed. 'Well we've got a week; we'll get him, Steve.' I'll make damn sure I do, Horton thought. 'I've instigated a check on Culven's land line and his mobile phone calls, and I've applied for a warrant to go through Culven's client files but I'll focus on the connection with

Thurlow for now, until something better shows up. I want to take a look at Thurlow's boat and talk to his staff tomorrow.'

'Good.' Uckfield drained his glass. 'I'd better be heading home, we've got the in-laws coming over for dinner. I'll brief Reg on the investigation.'

Reginald Dyer was the Chief Constable, and not one of Horton's fans.

Uckfield hesitated for a moment as if trying to make up his mind to speak. When he did, Horton almost wished he hadn't. 'Alison saw Catherine yesterday.'

'Oh?' Horton tried to look unconcerned but he didn't know if he succeeded. His heart skipped a beat as he thought of his wife and he felt his body tense.

'She thinks Catherine is seeing someone; it was just one or two remarks that she made. Andy, it was bound to happen. She's an attractive woman. And she thinks the marriage is over.'

'Right,' Horton replied. It was all he could do to get that word out. He stared straight ahead seeing nothing, hearing nothing. He tried to concentrate all his energy on remaining calm but it was almost impossible. A great searing fury assailed him.

'You OK? Andy?'

Horton forced himself to look at Uckfield. With a supreme effort he pulled himself up. 'Yeah,' he said keeping his voice steady, amazed he could even speak. Through the pain of rejection he registered Uckfield's concerned expression but felt only hatred.

'Look, I'd stay for a couple of drinks, only I can't.' Uckfield snatched a glance at his watch. 'I'm late. Some other time, eh? We'll go out on a blinder.'

Horton moved his mouth so that it resembled a smile. 'Yeah, some other time.'

He walked out with Uckfield and watched him climb into his car. With a toot he drove off. The hatred he had felt sitting in the pub and staring at Uckfield didn't abate but churned his gut. Uckfield had everything, a wife, family, home. And what did he have? A Harley Davidson and an old boat.

But it wasn't Uckfield he should hate he thought as he turned away. He had to concentrate his fury in the right place. He had to get even with whoever it was had wrecked his life. But he seemed no further forward with his investigations into Alpha One and Colin Jarrett. Still, patience, he urged himself. There had to be something in those files and he had a legitimate reason to go through them and ask Jarrett questions if necessary.

He wished he had the Harley but Malcolm Hargreaves had called earlier to say that there was a slight delay with it and he couldn't return it until the morning. His footsteps were heavy as he thought of Catherine and began to walk through the back streets of Portsmouth, passing the flats and tiny houses where he'd been pushed from pillar to post after his mother had walked out one chilly November morning and had never returned.

Shit! He wanted to do a ton. He wanted to roar away into oblivion. Uckfield's words resounded in his head. How long had Catherine been seeing someone? Who was he? How could she pick up with someone so quickly? It was as if their ten-year marriage counted for nothing. He dug his fingernails into the palms of his hand, oblivious of where he walked and the fog that enveloped him.

He had hoped. Even when he'd got that letter from her lawyers he had still hoped. But Uckfield was right; Catherine was a very attractive woman. There had been many at the station that had eyed her up but unless they had rank she wouldn't even smile at them. When he'd got his promotion to inspector she'd been over the moon.

And what about Emma? The thought of another man taking his place with his daughter made him feel sick. He knew he had to see Catherine, to try and reason with her? But what could he say except the same old thing; I didn't do it, you must believe me.

He tasted the bitterness in his mouth. It stayed with him all the way home, as did the anger. *Nutmeg* rocked to the tread of his footsteps as he removed the padlock. The hatch screeched as he pushed it back, setting his teeth on edge. His sleeping bag was still on the boom and would be damp by now, but he didn't care. How could he sleep anyway?

He lay on his bunk and stretched his hands behind his head. Then he flicked on the lamp to stare at Emma's photograph, experiencing the dull ache of missing her; recalling how she used to come running into their bedroom giggling and jump all over the bed. How Catherine used to scold her and how he would tickle her and jiggle her on his knees, making her screech with laughter for which he would get into further trouble for making his daughter 'too excited'. Now there was just the sound of a dog barking and the water slapping against the boat.

He frowned. Something was wrong. Something was different. His whole body tensed. He lay immobile, hardly breathing. There was no doubting it; Emma was not where she should have been. He always arranged the photograph at the exact angle where Emma's eyes were smiling at his when he awoke and now they looked beyond him to his right. Someone had moved Emma, which meant . . . Someone had been on his boat.

He sat bolt upright almost banging his head on the coach roof. Someone had broken in but it had been a very professional job. No lock had been tampered with, nothing disturbed. He wouldn't have known that anyone had been aboard if it hadn't been for Emma.

Slowly he swung off the bunk and, reaching into a locker, pulled out a pair of sailing gloves and began a minute inspection of the boat. It didn't take him long. He found it stowed away underneath his sail cover at the aft.

He pulled it out and stared at it, frowning; it was a slim, gold cigarette lighter. Who did it belong to? There was nothing on it to identify the owner, or was there? He peered at it wishing he had a magnifying glass. He could see some faint lettering, initials maybe, but they were so worn that he couldn't quite make them out. Someone had planted it with a purpose in mind, and he wasn't about to sit back and wait for that purpose to be revealed.

He climbed off the boat, taking care to look around. As far as he was aware there was no one watching him but then the fog was pretty thick. If anyone was watching him then they'd assume he was simply going to the toilet, or having a shower, which was exactly what he was doing. The lighter was safely tucked away inside his toilet bag.

He walked to the end of the pontoon. The fog swallowed up the sounds of the night completely leaving only the reboant foghorns to pierce the silence.

He slipped into the shower room and toilets. They were empty but swiftly he checked them all just to be certain. Then, entering the cubicle at the far end, he took the lighter, which was now enclosed in a sealed plastic bag, out of his toilet bag, opened the top of the toilet and placed it inside the cistern. He then took his time having a shower.

Outside he stood stock still as though he was savouring the night air, but he was checking for any movement, his ears and eyes straining for any sign that would tell him he was being watched. Nothing. The air was turbid and tasted of salt. He could hardly see in front of him as he made his way slowly and carefully back to his boat.

He lay on his bunk, staring into the dark. How had his intruder got in? He must have a key. It wouldn't be that difficult to get hold of one. The hatch was only fastened with a simple padlock. There wasn't much on the boat for anyone to steal so he'd never bothered to make it more secure. There were cameras in the marina and a code giving access on to the pontoons. The cameras probably wouldn't reveal much in the fog, always assuming they'd been pointing in this direction, and someone could easily have slipped through the gate along with another berth holder or behind one.

And why plant something on him now when he'd been here several weeks? But he knew the answer to that. Jarrett didn't want him sniffing around, which meant that he was on the right track. The thought cheered him.

But how did Jarrett know where to plant the lighter? Who knew he was living on his boat? Not Superintendent Underwood, his former boss in the Special Investigations Department, who could have been corrupt and had wanted that investigation into Alpha One to be compromised. Underwood was retired but he still had a pension to protect and wouldn't want him stirring up trouble. Someone could have told him. Someone at the station who was still in touch with him. For example, Dennings of the Vice Squad? But surely Dennings didn't know. Or perhaps he did and Horton's living arrangements and his estrangement from his wife were common knowledge in the station. But if that wasn't so then there were only three people who knew, four if you counted Catherine, but why would Catherine want to break in and plant a cigarette lighter on him? No, it couldn't be her. It had to be one of the others and until he found out, he could trust no one, not even Cantelli.

EIGHT

Friday

'How many people at the station know I'm living on the boat?' Horton asked Cantelli the next morning, as they headed for Oyster Quays and Thurlow's office.

'I think it's fairly common knowledge. Walters found out. Don't ask me who told him but you know what that means.'

He did. The whole of the Hampshire Police Service probably knew by now, so bang went his narrow list of suspects, but not necessarily his theory. Glancing at Cantelli he knew he had never seriously considered him one of them. But Dennings was a different matter.

'Why do you want to know?'

'No reason,' Horton replied airily and drew a sceptical look from Cantelli, which he chose to ignore. By the look of him Cantelli had spent as restless a night as he had done. 'Ellen still not talking to you?'

'No. I found out last night that Jaz Corinder told her mother she was on a sleep-over at Sophie's house. Neither girl returned to her own home on Tuesday night. Where the devil were they, Andy, and what were they up to?' Cantelli cried.

'Maybe Ellen wasn't with them.'

'Maybe. And that worries the hell out of me. If she wasn't, then where was she?'

'She'll tell you when she's ready,' Horton tried to comfort him but he could see that Cantelli wasn't convinced. Still, if anyone could get information from Ellen Cantelli, Horton was convinced that Charlotte could. Barney's wife understood children and adolescents better than anyone he knew. 'Let's try and concentrate on the case, Barney.'

'Yeah, OK.' Cantelli threw him a dubious glance.

As they made their way down the Plaza towards the sea, Horton could see over the heads of the crowds the masts of yachts crossing the harbour entrance and the top of the Isle of Wight ferry as it waited to berth. He felt a great deal of sympathy for Cantelli. He tried to imagine how he would feel if it were Emma. The answer was in the tightening of his stomach muscles and the ache around his heart.

He pushed open the door to Thurlow's office and climbed the stairs to reception where after a couple of minutes they were shown into a modern boardroom with a large glass-topped table and chrome armchairs.

The room was decorated in pale blue and Horton was immediately drawn to the two large arched shaped windows that overlooked the bustling harbour entrance and the town of Gosport beyond. Below him, moored up against the pontoon were three international racing yachts. The boardwalk was crowded with shoppers and tourists. It was another scorching day but this room, as the rest of the building, was mercifully air-conditioned.

'Thurlow likes to look at himself,' Cantelli said and Horton turned back to find Cantelli studying the photographs on the walls. There were several of Thurlow with clients at black tie dinners, Thurlow with celebrities, Thurlow on his boat with guests, and Thurlow with an athletic looking man sporting a marathon medal in front of a group of disabled children.

'Isn't this your father-in-law?' Cantelli pointed to a distinguished looking man in his late fifties standing beside Thurlow at a black tie presentation. Toby Kempton was holding a glass trophy and Roger Thurlow a jeroboam of champagne.

Horton read the caption underneath the photograph. 'Businessman of the Year 1992.' It was the year he had met Catherine. She had worked for her father then as a secretary and had since graduated to marketing manager for the internationally renowned manufacturer of sailing equipment.

Cantelli said, 'You heard from Catherine?'

He must have read his mind. That wouldn't have been difficult given the link. 'Only from her solicitor. She wants a divorce.' He said it evenly but his stomach was churning; now he understood perfectly why she'd filed for a divorce. 'She's found someone else.'

Cantelli looked shocked and Horton was grateful for that. But before either man could speak the door opened and a small man in his mid-fifties with overlong greying hair bustled in.

'I'm so sorry to keep you waiting gentlemen; I got caught on the phone. Charles Calthorpe.'

He spoke with a slight lisp. His eyes looked wary and there was a line of perspiration on his upper lip.

'Inspector Horton and this is Sergeant Cantelli.' Horton displayed his warrant card. The dark brown eyes studied him briefly and darted away as soon as Horton made contact with them. The handshake was moist and fleeting.

Calthorpe waved them into a seat and settled himself nervously. He seemed relieved when the door opened and a middle-aged woman, shaped like a pyramid, entered carrying a laden tray.

'Ah, coffee. Thank you, Mrs Stephens.' Calthorpe's slightly fleshy lips twitched in a half smile.

Horton caught the woman's eye. 'I understand you're Mr Thurlow's PA.' She started so violently that the coffee cups rattled and some coffee spilled on the tray she placed on the table. She flashed a look of alarm at Calthorpe who spoke for her.

'Mrs Stephens is very concerned about Roger's disappearance as are we all. I take it that's why you're here, Inspector?'

Mrs Stephens's face flushed a deep pink. She stammered something and scurried away. Calthorpe watched her go like a man who'd just seen the lifeboat roar passed him while his boat was sinking.

'Help yourself to milk, sugar and biscuits,' he said nervously.

Horton refrained from all three but Cantelli spooned in two sugars and helped himself to a Digestive. He removed his pen from behind his ear and extracted his notebook from his jacket pocket.

'When was the last time you saw Mr Thurlow?' Horton asked.

'Last Friday, when I left the office.'

'And what time was that, sir?'

'Just after six. Roger was going to his boat.' Calthorpe picked up his coffee and took a sip.

'Did he say where he was going for the weekend?'

'No.'

Calthorpe's eyes darted between them, and Horton got the impression of an insecure man underneath the self-important and agitated manner.

'Did you ever go with him?'

'Rarely, only when we were entertaining clients. I prefer wind over motor. I have my own small boat, a Bavaria 33.'

Horton wouldn't have described that as small. If Calthorpe wanted small he should come aboard *Nutmeg*! The directors must be taking a considerable amount out of the company for Thurlow to have a Mainship and Calthorpe a Bavaria.

'Where do you keep it, sir?'

Calthorpe looked surprised by the question and then a little annoyed. 'At Sparkes Yacht Harbour, Hayling Island. Why?'

'Did you go out over the weekend?'

'Yes, and before you ask I didn't see Roger. I came back Sunday night.' He picked up his spoon and began fiddling with it. Then seeing Horton's eyes on him he took a deep breath and put the spoon down. 'Look, Inspector, I don't know where Roger is. It's most inconvenient of him to go off like this. It's stretched us to the limit.'

Calthorpe looked about to say more then seemed to think better of it. Instead he pressed his lips together, wriggled a little and looked away. Obviously he hadn't spoken to Melissa Thurlow, or had he and that was why he was nervous? Had Melissa Thurlow told him that they suspected her husband of murder?

Horton left a silence, and just when it looked as though Calthorpe could bear it no longer asked, 'Did Mr Thurlow have any worries: health, financial, marital?'

'Not that I know of,' Calthorpe replied tersely.

'Has he been acting unusually, or was anything disturbing him?'

'Such as?'

'If I knew that I wouldn't need to ask, would I, sir?' Horton replied smiling. Calthorpe didn't seem to like it judging by his expression.

Rather crisply he answered, 'He seemed fine to me. Now I am rather busy.

'I understand that Michael Culven is the company's solicitor.'

Calthorpe had half risen. 'What's that got to do—'

'Mr Culven had an appointment with Roger Thurlow last Friday lunchtime, at the yacht club at Horsea Marina. Do you know what that meeting was about?'

Calthorpe sat down again. 'I've no idea.'

'Would Mrs Stephens know?' Horton pressed.

'I doubt it,' Calthorpe replied acerbically. 'I really don't see what Culven has to do with Roger—'

'He *is* your company lawyer, isn't he?'

'Well, yes, but I leave that sort of thing to Roger and Graham Parnham, our accountant and office manager. I'm the creative director, so the running of the business doesn't really concern me apart from the fact that we do good work for our clients. I leave most of the practical elements of running the business to Roger and Graham.'

Horton rose abruptly, surprising Cantelli and relieving Calthorpe. 'Thank you for your time and help, Mr Calthorpe. We won't hold you up any longer. If we could just have a word with Mr Parnham and Mrs Stephens.'

Parnham was out with the bank manager, so Mrs Stephens told them in her little office. She also told them that she had no idea why Roger had wanted to see Michael Culven.

'I think it was just a social call, they were fairly good friends,' she said stiffly. The door behind her, Horton guessed, led into Thurlow's office.

'Have you any idea where Mr Thurlow might be?'

'No I haven't, Inspector,' she replied, eyeing him warily. 'This is simply not like him at all.'

Horton asked her the same question he'd asked Calthorpe, if there had been anything troubling Thurlow, anything on his mind, or if he had been acting out of character, but she was shaking her head before he'd even finished the question.

'No, Roger was fine. There was nothing upsetting him.'

Nevertheless Horton could see there was a great deal upsetting Mrs Stephens. He smiled at her encouragingly and asked: 'When did you last see him?'

'On Friday night. I left here just after five thirty.'

'And he didn't say where he was going over the weekend?'

'Only out on his boat. He said he'd be back.' She hesitated. She seemed to have something more to say but wasn't sure how to say it. She looked at each of them in turn.

'Something troubling you, Mrs Stephens?'

'No. Nothing.' She pressed her lips together as if to prevent them from contradicting her.

Clearly there was something, but it was obvious she wasn't going to tell them what it was.

As they made their way back to the car, Cantelli said, 'Calthorpe's a funny little man. Very nervous I thought.'

'Highly strung, artistic type, I expect. I'm going to take a look at Thurlow's boat. You get over to the yacht club, Barney, see what you can find out about this meeting, and if anyone saw either man after last Friday lunchtime.'

His phone rang. It was Trueman.

'There's no evidence of Mrs Thurlow's fingerprints in Culven's house, guv. Only Culven's and Miss Filey's.'

So where had they conducted their affair? At Briarly House? It seemed a bit unlikely that she would risk it there when her husband could come home at any time, and when Culven's place was more appropriate, he being a bachelor. He could hardly see Mrs Thurlow having it away in the back of Culven's Mercedes. And where was the Mercedes? So far there had been no sighting of it.

Cantelli dropped him off at the Continental Ferry Port on his way out of the town. Horton located Sergeant Elkins of the Marine Unit and together they climbed on board the *Free Spirit*.

'This is exactly as you found it?' he asked Elkins, stepping into the central cabin.

'Yes, sir.'

It was beautifully furnished with soft blue upholstered cushions, which looked as though they had never been sat upon. In front of him was a mahogany table. There was nothing on it. Horton pushed open a door leading down into the galley. On the table there was an earthenware mug, a half drunk bottle of water, a Stanford's All Weather Chart revealing the blue of the Solent and the lighter blue and muddy orange of the Channel of Portsmouth Harbour and on top of the chart, a state of the art digital hand-held navigation system, manufactured by Kiltons. There was also a transparent ruler and a slim line gold ballpoint pen.

He crossed to the mug. It contained the dregs of what looked, and smelt, like coffee. Forensic would probably be able to tell him the brand, where the coffee had been grown, ground and sold.

'There's no sign of any struggle. I suppose it could have been cleaned up,' Elkins suggested.

'Someone would have to be master cleaner of the year to get it looking like this.'

Horton moved forward into one of the two sleeping cabins. This was clearly Thurlow's. Elkins took the other one.

Thurlow's navy blue sailing bag was on the bunk. Horton opened it and peered inside, a couple of pairs of shorts, T-shirts, underpants and socks. His shaving gear was still in the toilet bag, which he unzipped. Inside was the usual: toothpaste, razor, aftershave and shaving cream but then his fingers clasped something that wasn't so usual.

He pulled out a small bottle of tablets. They were prescribed to Roger Thurlow. Hypovase. He wondered what they were for; both Mrs Thurlow and Charles Calthorpe had said that Thurlow didn't have any health problems and although Thurlow might not have told Calthorpe, surely his wife would know if there was something wrong with him? Perhaps they weren't for anything serious and she hadn't thought it worth mentioning? He popped the bottle into a plastic evidence bag. They'd have a word with his GP.

He continued his search, moving into the tiny bathroom. Only a man's shower gel from the Body Shop, half used, hung in the shower tidy. Above the sink basin was a Perspex glass toothbrush holder. He could see no women's toiletries.

He bent down and pulled open the cupboard under the sink. Inside he found a bottle of household bleach from Waitrose, a tube of bathroom cleaner, and a couple of rags. As he made to straighten up something caught his eye. The bottom of the cupboard was laid with pale blue carpet tiles and he could see in the far right hand corner that one of them had curled slightly. Perhaps the damp had got to it he thought, or maybe the heat. Perhaps it hadn't been laid properly. In a boat costing over £200,000! Somehow he didn't think so.

He knelt and prised up the edge of the carpet tile. It came up remarkably easily; too easily Horton thought as he reached in and felt his fingers grip something. It was a pile of magazines. At first he thought they must have been used as lining, but what kind of boat fitters would use magazines to line a luxury yacht like this? Stretching forward he gently lifted them out.

The front cover of each of the three magazines sported naked couples; one of a man and woman, the other two of women locked in poses that left the reader in no doubt of their main activity. It didn't require any great leap of imagination to guess what was inside the covers.

He flicked quickly through the pages, though his experience in Special Investigations and the Vice Squad had already primed him for what he would see, hardcore porn that would never see the light of day on the top shelves of even the less discerning newsagents. These magazines were distributed privately and were smuggled into the country either from Germany or from Holland. And why he knew that was because they were the same sort of stuff that had been found on Woodard and which had led them to Alpha One and Jarrett.

He sat back on his heels, his mind racing and his heart pumping a little faster. No, this couldn't be linked to Jarrett; that was too much to hope for, surely? But there was a connection: Culven was both Jarrett's and Thurlow's solicitor; Thurlow's office was a stone's throw from Alpha One. Culven liked being caned; Thurlow was carrying hardcore porn; Jarrett was distributing it. OK, so the last was speculation but there were too many connections to be coincidence. Or was that just wishful thinking on his part? Was he so obsessed that he wanted Culven's death to be connected to Jarrett? He knew what Uckfield would say.

He heard Elkins give a soft whistle.

'Get me a large evidence bag, Dai,' Horton commanded.

Elkins returned promptly by which time Horton was back on deck holding the offending articles.

'Any sign of Thurlow's tender yet?'

Elkins shook his head. 'No and if it's not marked with the boat's name we might never find it. There are hundreds of dinghies lying around and tons of places it could be.'

Horton agreed. He called for a forensic team to go aboard Thurlow's boat then walked the few hundred yards to the large modern import control building where he asked to see Tom Maddox, the senior import and marine liaison officer.

A couple of minutes later Horton was standing in his office watching the cars being driven onto a ferry bound for France. Beyond it he could see the masts of the ships in Horsea Marina. He wondered how Cantelli was getting on.

Horton said, 'I need you to check out a yacht for me, Tom. Porn's involved.' He saw Maddox eye the evidence bag in his hand but he wasn't going to show it yet.

'What's she called?' Maddox waved him into a seat, folded his tall, lean frame into the chair opposite and pushed up his spectacles.

'The *Free Spirit.* She's in the secure compound.'

'I can't say I know the name.'

'Roger Thurlow's the owner. He's missing and we want to question him in connection with murder. You've probably heard about our body on the beach.'

Maddox swivelled his chair, his craggy features frowning as he thought. 'Thurlow. I don't know the name or the boat. Who's the dead man?'

'Michael Culven. He had a boat called *Otter.*'

'No. Doesn't ring any bells. I'll check them both out but I don't think we've ever stopped them.'

'Are you still keeping an eye on Jarrett?' Horton didn't really expect an honest answer. What he expected was the same reaction he'd got from Dennings, a warning to stay away.

Maddox raised his eyebrows but said, 'As far as we can tell he's clean.'

Horton sat forward. 'You and I both know he's not, Tom. He may not be bringing the porn in himself but he's involved in distributing it.'

Tom Maddox looked puzzled. 'There's no proof—'

'And you know why, because of me.'

'Look, Andy, we've got enough problems with drugs and illegal immigrants coming in. Jarrett's boat was stopped before Operation Extra and nothing was found on it. We kept an eye on him all the time the operation was live but it was dropped eight months ago.'

Yeah like me, Horton thought.

Maddox said, 'We were told it was finished.'

'And you always do what you're told?' Horton quipped.

Maddox grinned. 'No.'

'OK, so this might change your mind.' Horton thrust the bag across the desk. He watched Maddox turn it over and poke at the magazines through the plastic.

Horton said, 'Tell me where that comes from?' He knew the answer but he wanted to hear Maddox say it.

'Germany, Holland.' Maddox glanced up. 'What's the connection with Jarrett?' But Horton didn't have to tell him. Maddox answered his own question. 'You think Jarrett is using this guy Thurlow and was using Culven to bring the stuff in?'

'Looks like it to me.'

Maddox sat back. Horton watched the thoughts race across his face. Behind the steel framed glasses he saw Maddox's eyes glance back at the porn. Then he pursed his lips together and said, 'What do you want me to do?'

'Just keep an eye on Jarrett for now. Don't stop him but log his movements. I want to know when he goes out on his boat, who he goes out with and where he goes. I think there's a connection between Culven's death, Thurlow's disappearance and Jarrett but I've got nothing definite at the moment.'

Maddox nodded.

Horton said, 'Let's keep this between ourselves, Tom. I was set up once, if Jarrett gets wind of this we'll never find anything.'

'You can count on me. I always thought that accusation against you was baloney.'

Horton walked back to the station feeling that he was beginning to get somewhere at last, and not just with Colin Jarrett, but Culven's murder. He logged the porn magazines into the incident room and asked for them to be sent for fingerprinting. Then he summoned Marsden.

'I found these on Thurlow's boat.' He held out the tablets. 'Get along to the GP and find out why Thurlow was taking them.'

He headed for the canteen where he bought himself a packet of sandwiches and took them to his office. He stared at the telephone and then glanced at his watch. Where was Catherine now? Would she be at work? She often took time off in August to be with Emma during the summer holidays. *They* had often taken time off together to be with their daughter and to go sailing or camping.

His fingers swivelled to the framed photograph on the corner of his desk. He picked it up. He was crouched down behind her, his arms encircling her slender body; they were on the deck of *Nutmeg*. The wind had caught her hair blowing it across her face and he was laughing. My God, once he had actually laughed. He replaced the photograph and picked up the telephone.

'Catherine Horton,' he asked.

'I'm afraid she's not in today. Can anyone else help you?'

'No thanks.'

His palms were wet with sweat and his heart was beating rapidly. Should he call her at home? Would it be better to take a chance and go out there? His phone rang. It was Malcolm with his Harley. He made for the car park and took delivery of the machine, back in perfect working order. As Malcolm drove away Cantelli pulled in and he told him about the porn and the tablets.

Cantelli said, 'Perhaps that's how Thurlow can afford an expensive boat and that house, by smuggling porn.'

'And Thurlow killed Culven because he got too greedy and asked for more to feed his sexual preferences. Thurlow didn't want to pay up. Culven had become a liability.'

'And the affair?'

'Coincidental. We've got access to Culven's finances now. We'll be able to analyse his transactions and see how much he paid for his caning and who he paid it too.'

'Do you think Mrs Thurlow knows about the porn?'

'She could do. Culven could have told her. How did you get on at the yacht club?'

'The barman confirmed that Culven and Thurlow were there last Friday lunchtime. He says they used to have lunch together quite often. Culven was also a frequent evening visitor, often for dinner, usually alone, but occasionally with clients. He says Culven was a quiet chap, kept himself to himself, not like Thurlow who seems to be the life and soul of the party. A real Jolly Roger.' Horton saw a smile brighten Cantelli's troubled face for a moment and he knew there was more to come. 'And the barman recalls Culven coming in on Tuesday evening. He was alone. He had a meal and left just after eight thirty.'

And that was the last time anyone had seen their murdered man alive, except for the murderer, of course.

'Find out what food they served Tuesday evening and check it with Doctor Clayton's findings on stomach contents.'

'Already done,' said Cantelli waving his notepad.

'Did Culven tell the barman where he was going?'

Cantelli raised his bushy eyebrows. 'Do you want jam on it?'

Horton smiled. Would be nice, he thought.

NINE

He wasn't smiling an hour later when he was told there was a delay in getting the warrant to obtain Culven's client files and Frances Greywell was refusing to hand them over. She had to protect her firm's reputation and her client's interests, so Cantelli told him after speaking to her on the telephone. Damn, that meant they might not have access to them until Monday morning. Two whole days wasted. They may not have a warrant to extract the files but Horton had sent Walters and another DC into Framptons to question the staff.

The team questioning Culven's neighbours hadn't unearthed any regular visitors to Culven's house, man or woman, except for his cleaner. Culven's sister was in New Zealand and, it appeared, apart from her Culven had no family and no friends.

The fingerprinting unit confirmed the prints on the pornographic magazines matched Roger Thurlow's. After briefing Uckfield, Horton handed the magazines over to Dennings and the Vice Squad to trace their origin. Horton said nothing to Uckfield about his visit to Maddox or his ideas that Thurlow and Culven were involved with Jarrett. He doubted Uckfield would appreciate it.

He felt restless. He tried to settle down to clear some of the paperwork that had been building up but couldn't, and even checking in with Trueman in the incident room didn't ease his agitation. He wanted action, or at least activity that didn't involve reading and shuffling paper. Everything that could be done on the Culven case was being done so he decided to pursue the Thurlow line.

It was late afternoon when he climbed the steps to the office at Horsea Marina. Someone might have seen Thurlow on his boat last Friday, and the lockmaster might have seen him go out. It was worth checking. He showed his warrant card to a young woman with fair hair and a worried expression, and asked to have a word with the lockmaster to check on procedures.

'Of course,' she agreed with alacrity. 'I hope there's nothing wrong?'

'No. Just routine,' but he could see she wasn't convinced. 'Do you know the *Free Spirit* owned by Roger Thurlow?'

She shook her head. 'No, I haven't been here long. One of the others might know him.'

'Perhaps you could tell me where he keeps his boat?'

'Yes.' She reached for a file and, quickly thumbing through it, found the pontoon and berth number.

He asked for the security number to get on to the pontoon, then she showed him into the lock control room. A bulky balding man with a bird tattoo on the side of his neck was sitting in front of a large cream-coloured console with red and green buttons biting into a sandwich the size of a small loaf.

To Horton's enquiry he said, 'Are you kidding mate? You couldn't see the end of your nose on Friday evening, and if he went out in that fog then he's a ruddy fool. Though a lot of them are when it comes to the water. What happened to you then, get into a fight?'

'Something like that.' Horton thought he should wear a placard saying, 'I got knocked off my bike.' He gazed across the lock at the houses directly opposite that faced Portchester Lake. It might be worth talking to the occupants.

'Of course we were on free flow Friday night,' the lock-master mumbled through a mouthful of bread and ham. 'You know what that is?'

Horton did. It meant the tide was at the right height to allow a boat to free flow through the lock without having to use the gates. 'What time was this?'

The lockmaster consulted a chart on his wall. 'Between 6.44 a.m. and 9.14 a.m. and again between 7.19 p.m. and 10.04 p.m.'

If Thurlow had taken his boat out that evening after 7.30 p.m. he wouldn't have needed to radio up. That factor, combined with the fog, would have meant he could have slipped out without anyone seeing him. But perhaps he had stayed in the marina overnight and gone out over the weekend?

'Did you see the *Free Spirit* at all over the weekend?'

'Can't say I did. She might have slipped through though. We only log boats out if they're vacating a berth for one or more nights.'

'Can you check,' Horton asked, squeezing the impatience from his voice.

He consulted a clipboard. 'No, mate, nothing there.'

Horton could ask Thurlow's fellow berth holders. The radio crackled into life. Below, Horton could see a sleek motorboat edging its way into the lock.

The lockmaster continued, 'Of course in this hot weather, during the day, the world and his wife are coming in and out of here like it was a motorway service station.'

Horton knew that. He recalled the days when he, Catherine and Emma had come through here on his father-in-law's yacht. 'Could you give me the free flow times for the weekend until Tuesday evening, please?' He didn't know what relevance it had, probably none, but he might as well have the information while he was here. He guessed that Thurlow had moored up elsewhere in the Solent.

The lockmaster stretched out and handed across a long thin leaflet. Then he screwed the paper sandwich bag into a tight ball and tossed it into a bin in the far corner by the open door.

Horton said, 'Do you know a Michael Culven, owns a Sealine 25?'

'What's the name of the boat?'

'*Otter*.'

'Doesn't ring a bell.'

Had Culven sold it? Horton left him pushing his buttons and headed back towards the boardwalk and the bridge head that led on to Thurlow's pontoon. He walked steadily past the gleaming yachts and motorboats looking for occupants, but they were all deserted. He guessed that many of the boat owners would be down from London, and other parts of the country, later that evening in readiness for the weekend sailing. He wondered if he'd ever be able to afford a boat that had more than just one cabin and even possibly a separate head! Uckfield had managed it but then Steve Uckfield had managed most things.

He came to a halt at the empty berth where the *Free Spirit* should have been, and couldn't believe his luck! He had wanted a reason to question Jarrett and he'd been given one. Opposite where the *Free Spirit* should have been was Jarrett's sleek motorboat. Now he was convinced that Thurlow was working with Jarrett and that both were involved in smuggling pornography. He didn't recall seeing Thurlow enter Alpha One, when he and Dennings had been watching it, or Culven come to that, but then Thurlow and Culven didn't need to be members, they both had boats here. It would have been easy to transfer the pornography between them.

Even better, Jarrett was on board. The hunch that had brought him out here when he should have been reading reports had paid off.

He made to hail Jarrett when he emerged from the cabin. As Jarrett took in his arrival, Horton saw his eyes flick beyond him, to the car park, as if he was expecting someone.

'I could call this harassment,' Jarrett said, climbing down on to the pontoon. Obviously Horton wasn't going to be invited on board.

'You could. I call it questioning a possible witness to a murder.' That shook him.

'What murder?'

'The body found on the beach, Wednesday morning.'

'What's that got to do with me?'

'He was your solicitor.'

Jarrett's head came up and Horton could have sworn he saw alarm in his eyes.

'Michael's been killed?'

Horton was about to say as if you didn't know but something stopped him. Despite what he wanted to think Jarrett looked genuinely shocked and unnerved.

'Where were you between nine and midnight Tuesday night?'

'You know where. In the hospital. You saw me leaving Wednesday morning, remember?'

He did. 'Didn't you tell me you were rammed in the early hours of Wednesday morning?'

'Maybe I got the time wrong.'

'I'll check with traffic,' Horton said, reaching for his phone. 'I take it you reported the incident to the police like any good citizen.'

Jarrett looked nervous and said hastily, 'I remember now I was on my boat until eleven thirty.'

Horton suppressed a smile and slowly put his phone back in his jacket pocket. Was Jarrett telling the truth? Did he have a motive for killing Culven? Yes, perhaps the same one he'd voiced to Cantelli earlier: Culven had got greedy and wanted a bigger share of the profits and Jarrett wasn't having it.

'Anyone with you?'

'What do you mean?'

Horton remained silent and waited. Jarrett glared at him. After a moment he spat, 'No.'

He was lying about that but the traffic accident would be easy to check out. Horton didn't press it. For now. 'How well do you know Roger Thurlow?'

'Who?' It was clear to Horton that he didn't know him. He felt a stab of disappointment.

'Your neighbour.' He jerked his head in the direction of the vacant berth opposite.

Jarrett retrieved a packet of cigarettes from the top pocket of his loose fitting shirt and extracted a cigarette. 'Is that his name? I've said the odd thing to him, nice day, you going out.'

Horton watched him light up. Jarrett tossed back his head and let out a thin stream of smoke.

'Was he on his boat on Friday evening?'

'Didn't see him.'

'You were here?'

'Got back from the Isle of Wight about four o'clock, why?'

'And what time did you leave your boat that night?'

'Look what is all this?'

Horton remained silent.

'I don't know. I didn't look at the clock.'

Horton held Jarrett's discontented stare. Then almost casually he said, 'We found Thurlow's boat on the East Winner on Wednesday morning. He wasn't on board. Do you know where he is?'

'No.' Jarrett drew impatiently on his cigarette and then seeming to have got bored with it stubbed it out and flicked the butt into the water with the toe of his leather deck shoes.

'Did you see the boat go out over the weekend, or on Tuesday evening?'

'No.' Jarrett dashed a glance at his watch.

'Expecting someone?'

'No.' But Jarrett looked decidedly uncomfortable.

'Was Roger Thurlow a member of Alpha One?'

An angry flush spread up Jarrett's face. 'Sod off, Horton.'

'What about Michael Culven?'

'Go screw yourself.'

Horton marched down the pontoon feeling Jarrett's hostile glare following him. He'd unnerved Jarrett. Good. Make the bugger sweat. The pieces didn't quite fit together yet but they would.

Marsden was waiting for him when he got back.

'Thurlow's GP says he was suffering from hypertension, hence the Hypovase tablets. His last prescription was issued a fortnight ago.'

So something Mrs Thurlow would have known about. Horton cast his mind back to that first interview. Why did she lie when she said that her husband had no health problems?

'Have we got Culven's telephone records?'

'Yes, sir. I've started to go through them but there's nothing unusual as yet.' Marsden replied.

'Keep looking.'

'The warrant's come in, sir, for Frampton's.'

Horton glanced at his watch. It was too late now to visit the solicitors. 'First thing tomorrow, Marsden collect all Culven's client files for the last six months and bring them back here.'

'It's Saturday, sir. There won't be anyone in the office.'

'Then find someone. I want those files on my desk by noon tomorrow.' He was damned if he was going to wait around until Monday.

Marsden dismissed, Horton sat back and stretched out his legs. His back was aching from his accident. The only light in his office now was from the lamp on his desk. He could hear the duty CID officer in the main office talking quietly into the telephone.

There was little more he could do tonight but still he lingered, pushing bits of paper around his desk, reviewing files and clearing up odds and ends, all the time his subconscious mind working away on something completely different. Finally, he could put it off no longer.

God, how his heart was going! Would Emma pick up the telephone? Would he hear his daughter's voice? And if

Catherine answered what was he going to say to her? That he loved her and wanted her back? But it was ringing and ringing. Just as he was about to give up it was answered.

'Hello?'

It was a man's voice. Horton felt his throat go dry and his body tense.

'Hello? Who is it?'

Horton slammed down the receiver so hard that he thought he'd broken the damn thing. He swore softly. Then he sprang from his seat, pulled on his leathers and stormed out of his room, almost colliding with Marsden who jumped back alarmed.

'Inspector!'

'Not now!' Horton bellowed, as he swept through the detention area like a tornado.

He jumped on to his Harley and roared the machine into action, forgetting all about his stiff neck and bruised body. He sped out of Portsmouth like a man possessed. The great rage swept through him just as it had as a child. He didn't know how else to deal with the pain. Then he had wanted to lash out at a world that had hurt him. Now his instinct was just as strong. Catherine had abandoned him. She, like his mother, had tossed him aside like an old dress.

He raced along the motorway oblivious of speed limits, oblivious of the fact that he could kill himself, weaving in and out of cars and lorries, not caring. All he cared about was getting to Emma, getting her away from that man. No other man was going to take his place with his daughter. His mother and Catherine may have betrayed him but he wouldn't let them take Emma from him; he'd die first.

Catherine's car was on the driveway. The windows at the front of the house were shut. He hammered on the door. The neighbours' blinds twitched. He hammered again.

'Catherine, I know you're in there. Let me in, damn you!'

More blinds twitched and he heard a door open somewhere to his right.

'Catherine! Catherine!'

A cough from his right and, 'Andy . . .'

Horton rounded on the small, bald headed man. Eric Smith, blast him.

'Er . . . they're not in,' Eric stammered.

Horton stepped forward and Eric stepped back.

'They went out about fifteen minutes ago.' He licked his lips nervously, his eyes darting about.

His words penetrated Horton's fury and desperately he tried to get a hold on himself. It took all his powers of self-control. He felt a wave of sickness. 'Where?' he croaked.

'I don't know. They were dressed up.'

'They? Who was with her? Who was with my wife?' Horton stepped forward and Eric edged back on to his lawn and nearer the safety of his own front door.

'I don't know—'

'Damn it, Eric, who was she with?'

Eric looked at Horton's rigid body and clenched fists and swallowed hard. Horton saw Eric glance at his wife, Daphne, who had come out to support him, telephone in her hand ready to summon help. They'd had to once when Catherine had thrown him out and he'd stood hammering on the door half the night. Horton took a deep breath and tried to still his racing heart and retain his fury. Slowly he said, 'What's he look like, Eric?'

'Stocky, balding, suntanned. I don't know who he is.'

'What car does he drive?'

'A BMW, red, seven series. I don't know the number, honest, I've never looked.'

Bollocks, thought Horton, Eric and Daphne spent hours spying on their neighbours, they seemed to have nothing better to do with their empty lives. But he wasn't going to press him. His anger was subsiding and in its place came a rising sense of despair and even self-pity. He needed information and threatening Eric was no way to get it.

'How long has he been going out with Catherine?' he asked, making an enormous effort at control.

'I don't know if he is.'

'How long?'

'About three weeks. Well, that's how long the car's been around here. Now I must go.' Eric had retreated as far as his front door but Horton had followed him. Three weeks. Long enough to get into Catherine's bed and get to know his daughter.

'What's his name?'

'I only know it's Ed. Now I must go.' And with that he slammed the door.

Horton turned, his fury spent and climbed on to his Harley. Slowly he headed back to Portsmouth. What was the point? But there must be a point, there had to be. He couldn't give up now. There was still time. There must be time. But it was running out fast. Unless he got to the truth soon he would lose them both, probably forever. He headed for his boat, stopping at the shop on the corner of Fort Cumberland Road.

He lay on his berth as the fog closed in around him and stared at the bottle of whisky he'd just bought. It had been a long time since alcohol had touched his lips and then too much had, day after day, night after night, helping him to blot out the pain of betrayal and rejection; nullifying his senses. He didn't want to feel that pain again. He wanted oblivion. Soon Emma would forget him; soon Emma would have a new daddy, soon life wouldn't be worth living. Slowly he reached out a hand. Blast Catherine. Sod them all. His fingers curled around the bottle and he lifted it to his lips.

TEN

Saturday

He was running. The tunnel was closing in around him, the pinprick of light was fading; soon it would be gone. There would be no way out. Then a door appeared on his right. He pushed against it but it wouldn't budge. He tried harder but still it refused to open, and all the time a tune was playing in his head. The tune was getting louder.

His body was drenched with sweat and yet he was shivering. His breath was coming in gasps and someone was hammering inside his head. Slowly he surfaced from the fog of sleep and nightmares. He fumbled for the torch, found it and switched it on, then reached for his phone and growled into it.

'We've got another body, Inspector,' the voice on the other end said.

Horton pulled himself together. 'Who? Where?'

'Warlingham Tower, Inspector. Don't know who, but scene-of-crime officers are on their way, and so is Doctor Clayton.'

'What about DCI Uckfield?'

'He's not at home. I've tried his mobile but it's switched off. I left a message.'

'I'm on my way. Give Cantelli a call, will you. Ask him if he's not doing anything special, like sleeping, to meet me there.' He glanced at his watch; it was almost one o'clock.

He switched on the lamp filling the pokey cabin with subdued light. His head felt terrible. He reached for his water and then he saw it: the small bottle, which was still full of the amber liquid. It had taken him all his will power to resist it but he had. He felt a sense of personal satisfaction that he hadn't given in. Three months ago it would have been a very different story. It was a measure of how far he'd come. Despite extreme provocation he had resisted.

He should feel proud, but all he could feel was pain because he couldn't stop thinking of Catherine. What was she doing now? Was she in bed with this Ed, making love to him? And Emma? Oh God, was she in her pink bedroom with ballerinas on the wall, with her teddies and dolls, sleeping? Or was she awake listening to Mummy and wondering what she was doing? He felt nausea rise up in him and wanted to retch. Quickly he took a deep breath and pulled on his trousers. Think of the body, think of the case, think of anything but Emma.

He wrenched the T-shirt over his head, and, as he stepped over his running gear, he began to feel grateful to the corpse for rescuing him from his torments. He pulled on his leathers and emerged into the foggy night.

Warlingham was about eight miles to the east of Portsmouth on the Chichester Road. Once it had been a thriving hamlet but all that was left now was the tower, a farm, a church, and a large cemetery that bordered the shore. To the east of Warlingham the shore led round to the village of Emsworth and to the west the island of Hayling.

He indicated off the motorway and sensed, rather than saw, the turn-off, which led down a narrow, twisting country lane towards the ruined tower and beyond it to the shore. He pulled up behind a police car, its blue lights flashing eerily in the fog.

He had a quick word with the constable at the entrance to the tower, logged in, stepped into a scene suit and ducking under the tape hovered inside. A shiver ran down his spine. Whatever this place had been used for in the past it carried evil. How anyone could attempt to make love in here — which was what the young couple who had discovered the body had been doing — was a mystery to him.

Arc lights had been fixed up inside the tower, throwing into harsh spotlight the vestiges of human activity: empty cans of lager and beer, cigarette packets, condoms and other rubbish.

'You're going to have a field day sifting through this lot, Phil,' he said to the lean stooping man beside him.

'Yeah, judging by the number of condoms alone we'll be recording the semen traces and DNA of half the male population of Portsmouth,' he muttered through the white mask which, like Horton's, was covering his nose and face.

Horton stepped forward into the tower, but not too far; he didn't want to disturb the scene any more than was necessary. Besides he didn't need to go far to see, in the corner, the hunched body of a man; decomposing and partially consumed by the wildlife. His empty stomach heaved at the sight, never mind the smell. How the lovers could have missed that smell he didn't know, probably too consumed with their passion, he suspected. His stomach didn't only protest at the physical manifestations of the dead man but that his life had ended in such a place and in such a way. This death struck him as more pathetic and cruel than the corpse on the beach; maybe it was because the body lay hunched in a foetal position. Or perhaps it was because of the way it was clothed.

The purple dress stretched around the rotting flesh, the pale white flowers on it hardly visible for the crawling maggots. The black fishnet stockings and white shoes were the garb of a tart. That a man's life — and it was a man — could be so summarily dismissed and discarded here like this, left like rubbish, filled Horton with anger. It was good to feel anger at something other than Catherine's betrayal.

Peering down into the contorted face of the man, he recognised him, despite the fact that the maggots, flies, and other insect life, not to mention the rats, had begun to feast on it. It had to be Roger Thurlow. He hardly had time to digest this when a low whistle came from behind him and he turned to find Cantelli standing in the entrance.

Horton said, 'Lovers found him.'

'Blimey, I bet that put them off their stroke. Is it Thurlow?' Cantelli moved forward and peered across at the body. Horton saw him wince at the gruesome sight. 'What's he doing dressed like that? Thurlow a transvestite!'

'Perhaps it's the reason why Melissa Thurlow stopped loving him and looked for an affair elsewhere.'

It seemed to fit. But there was a lot more that didn't. So far no one had given any hint that Thurlow liked playing away from home with other women, or men come to that, though the pornography had indicated that Thurlow had some peculiar tastes when it came to sex. But he was jumping ahead of himself. They had yet to confirm the identity of the victim so he had better save the theorising until later.

Cantelli glanced at the body, then away again. 'Could he have placed that cord around his own neck and hanged himself to get an erection?'

A long, thin white cord lay stretched out from the body's neck. 'He could have done if there was anything to hang himself by.' Horton tilted his head upwards. If it had been a clear night he would have seen the stars. It had to be strangulation like Culven. He shuddered. 'This place gives me the creeps.'

'So it should,' Cantelli replied. 'It's called Devil's Tower because of the wild orgies that were held here years ago. It was part of Warlingham House once, ruined in the civil war. One of Charles I's mistresses used to live there. Charlotte told me.'

'You didn't wake her up just to ask her that?'

'No. She was already awake like me.' His expression clouded over and Horton guessed they had been worrying about Ellen. He felt for them. When Emma had an infection and raging temperature, and they suspected meningitis, he thought he was going to die with worry.

Horton turned at the sound of a soft West Country accent greeting the PC outside. A couple of seconds later

Doctor Clayton appeared at the entrance to the tower. He thought she looked about eighteen in her jeans and sweatshirt before she stepped into the scene suit.

He said, 'We'll be outside.'

She nodded, already absorbed in her work.

'I don't know how she does that job,' Horton said.

'Me neither,' replied Cantelli with feeling.

Uniform were arriving with more lights. Horton climbed out of his scene suit and nodded to the forensic photographer who had just arrived.

Cantelli said, 'The nearest house is about half a mile away, back on the main road to Emsworth. I shouldn't think anyone would have seen anything suspicious.'

'*If* the body was brought in that way.'

He saw Cantelli look at him sharply and explained. 'The sea is not fifty yards away beyond the tower, and on a high tide you can get in quite close to the shore.'

'You mean someone was on board with Thurlow?'

'It's possible.'

'Anyone in mind?'

Horton thought, Jarrett could have done it. He said, 'Let's see what Doctor Clayton has to say first.'

A couple of minutes later she emerged from the tower. Horton nodded the forensic photographer and the scene-of-crime officers in. Doctor Clayton pulled off her gloves and threw them into her case. 'I think I can say with some confidence that he's dead, though cause of death is a little difficult at the moment; too much decomposition, and the wildlife have had rather a good go at him.'

Horton said, 'How long?'

'Judging by the state of decomposition, and the weather, I would say about six or seven days. I'll know more once I get him on the slab.'

Horton looked at Cantelli and could see he was thinking along the same lines. This tied in with Thurlow's disappearing act. But if this was Thurlow, and he was almost certain it was, then that would mean he was killed before Culven.

Did Culven kill Thurlow so that he could be free to be with Melissa Thurlow? If so, who had killed Culven? He knew what Uckfield would say: Melissa Thurlow. And maybe he was right Horton thought with disappointment. The pornography and the fact that Thurlow's boat was kept near Jarrett's could, after all, be simply coincidences. But he felt so sure that something was going on.

He said, 'Was he killed here?'

'Sorry, Inspector, I can't help you there at the moment.' She paused in divesting herself of the scene suit. 'I'll do the PM tomorrow morning, first thing. Say eight thirty.'

'Thanks.'

He caught Cantelli yawning.

'I'm sorry to have dragged you out, Barney.'

'I'm glad you did. It was helpful to see him, poor soul.'

'Go home. I'll stay until the body is removed.'

'You sure?' Cantelli yawned again.

'Yes.'

Horton tried Uckfield's mobile once more, but there was still no answer. He left a message and waited for a while to see if Taylor had anything new to say about the scene-of-the-crime, but there was too much to sift through for instant answers. He saw the body removed to the mortuary, then climbed on his bike and headed home. He tried to get some sleep but soon knew that it was hopeless. At five o'clock he got up, showered and changed and headed into work. He had a feeling it was going to be a very long day but he didn't mind that. Work would distract him.

By the look of him Uckfield had also been awake all night. The big man looked washed out and hung over. Wherever he had been it had been quite a party, but Horton wasn't foolish enough to say so.

'Another bloody murder!' Uckfield snarled, pulling out a chair and flopping down opposite Horton across the table in the canteen. 'Just what I need.'

Horton refrained from saying he guessed that their victim could have done without it too. Instead he said, 'I think it's Thurlow but we won't know for certain until later this morning. I'm sending Somerfield out to Briarly House to warn Mrs Thurlow and stay with her if she needs her, but my experience of that lady is she won't want her there. If it is Thurlow, then he was killed before Culven. So we start again.'

'Could she have killed them both?' Uckfield asked hopefully, looking up from his black coffee.

Horton considered this. 'Why kill her lover?'

'How the hell do I know?' Uckfield snapped.

Horton raised his eyebrows. He'd only been posing a theoretical question; he didn't expect an answer. Definitely touchy this morning. He sipped his coffee and remained silent. After a moment Uckfield let out a sigh and his lips twitched in apology, but Horton could see how forced it was and how much it cost him to keep control of his temper, which at the best of times had never been even.

'Who else have we got in the frame?'

Horton wasn't going to tell him about Jarrett. He knew what the reaction would be.

'There must be others, you must have some idea!'

Horton felt the question to be an accusation of his incompetence. 'We'll need to start digging into Thurlow's affairs,' he replied stiffly.

'Then you'd better get a big shovel and do it quick.' Uckfield tossed back his coffee and scraped back his chair.

Horton sat for a moment longer staring into his coffee. Then, after checking into the incident room, he returned to his office where he spent the next few hours sifting through the files on Culven's murder, and reading the summary of statements that Trueman had compiled for him, looking for anything out of the ordinary or some commonality between the two men's deaths. All he could find was that they knew each other. Both bodies had been dumped close to the sea, and both had Melissa Thurlow and Colin Jarrett in common.

It was just after two o'clock when he collected Cantelli and they made their way to the mortuary. They found Doctor Clayton in her office. She looked tired.

'At first glance it appeared he was strangled,' she said. Her office looked as though a tornado had swept through it: papers were scattered across her desk and files littered the floor. A bookcase crammed with heavy volumes filled the wall to his left, and behind her hung a large portrait of a man executed in oils. He was in his fifties and in modern dress; Horton thought he looked vaguely familiar. On her desk, apart from the papers, there was a telephone, flat screen computer and three photographs in frames, facing away from him.

Cantelli asked, 'Do you think he was involved in some kind of sexual game that went wrong?'

'Auto-erotic asphyxia, deliberately restricting oxygen to the brain to enhance an orgasm. The way he was dressed might suggest that but even if he had indulged in such an activity before his death there is no evidence of semen, or that he had sex with anyone immediately prior to his death. The cord was placed around his neck after his death.'

'To make us think that he'd been involved in sex games?'

She shrugged. 'Possibly, but he died of asphyxiation like our other victim; this time I would say he's been suffocated with a plastic bag. It was difficult to tell because of the decomposition but I found some evidence of petechial haemorrhages on his shoulder and on the front of the chest, which hadn't been eaten by the wildlife. That's where I would expect to find them if a plastic bag had been placed over his head and held there until he died.'

'No signs of being knocked out, or beaten about the head?' asked Cantelli, chewing and jotting down notes.

'None whatsoever. You're wondering how a grown man, and a fairly fit one, could allow someone to put a plastic bag over him and suffocate him.'

Cantelli nodded. 'Something like that.'

'Which indicates he might already have been unconscious when it was done,' said Horton.

She gave him a rueful smile. 'Yes. I've sent his organs for analysis and a blood sample to histology, so if there is any sign of a drug, I'll let you know.'

'You could try looking for Hypervase. I found a bottle of the tablets on his boat. They'd been prescribed for hypertension. If someone had given him an overdose of those would it have induced a coma?'

'It certainly would.'

'Was he killed in the tower, Doctor, or was his body dumped there?' Horton repeated the question he'd asked her at the scene.

'The body had been moved. We're still doing the tests to see if we can pick up any traces of fibre or anything else to indicate where he might have been killed but he wasn't killed in the tower.'

That bore out what Phil Taylor had told him earlier. The undergrowth in and around the tower, and the disturbance of the debris in the tower, had both shown evidence of something being dragged over it and recently. Taylor couldn't say what but the description he had given Horton of the pattern of disturbance sounded remarkably like a tender.

'What about time of death?' Horton had once been given a lecture in forensic entomology in great detail by an enthusiastic and rather brutal pathologist when he had been a young and very green policeman attending one of his first post mortems. He hoped Gaye Clayton wasn't going to repeat it.

'Difficult to say exactly, but judging from the insect life feeding on the body, and the lifecycle of the maggots when the body was discovered, I would say they were just beginning the second stage of pupation. So, as I said at the scene, about six to seven days, which puts us somewhere near early hours of Saturday morning.' She swung gently in her chair. 'It's a bit different from the other body, isn't it?'

Horton eyed her keenly, interpreting her meaning. 'You mean this man was killed, transported and hidden, whereas our body on the beach, Michael Culven, was killed not far from where he was found and in full view.'

She nodded.

Horton continued. 'Which means it could be two killers, or one killer wanting us to think it is two.'

'Huh?' Cantelli enquired.

Horton explained: 'The killing of the first victim had some of the imprints of a disorganised offender: body left in full view and at, or near the death scene; sudden violence in the manner of strangulation; depersonalising the victim by bludgeoning his face. Whereas our second victim was hidden, he was killed elsewhere and moved to the tower — the profile of an organised offender.'

'Maybe the tower has some significance?' Cantelli ventured.

Horton didn't think so. He thought it was just a convenient place to dump a body, especially if done so from the sea, in the dark and fog. '*If* it is the same killer then I think this murder was carefully planned and that Culven either saw something that could betray the killer and therefore had to be silenced, or Culven's death was used as a delaying tactic. I keep recalling the way Culven was laid out. There has to be some symbolic reference in that.'

'You mean like he was on a cross?' Doctor Clayton said.

'Yes. Almost as if Culven was a sacrifice.' But sacrifice to what? Their second body might not have been discovered in that tower for a long time if it hadn't been for those lovers. An idea was beginning to form in Horton's mind, which he didn't much care for, mainly because it didn't fit with his theories on Jarrett being the possible killer.

Doctor Clayton said, 'If they are connected then your killer must be a clever and imaginative character.'

Horton agreed. There was no set pattern to this case, no easy profiling. This man was clever enough to conduct two murders that appeared completely different while trying to make them look similar by strangulation and the sexual implications.

The door opened and a young man in a white coat entered. 'The images you wanted, Doctor Clayton.' He stretched out a folder.

She gave him a smile before handing the folder to Horton. 'You'll find dental images, DNA breakdown and fingerprints in there. That should give you enough to identify him. I'll let you know as soon as I have anything on the organ analysis and from histology. Now I'm going to have to throw you out. I'm whacked and I want to get some sleep.'

Neither of them objected. As soon as they got back to the station Cantelli hurried off to check out the fingerprints with the Fingerprint Bureau. Horton had barely stepped inside his office when his mobile rang.

'What the devil do you think you're playing at, Andy, coming here and shouting and swearing at the neighbours?'

Christ! Catherine. His heart went into overdrive. He hadn't expected this though he might have known Eric and Daphne would go blabbing about his outburst last night. He kicked his door shut and turned his back on the CID office as he said, 'I didn't swear at—'

'It's over, Andy. Our marriage is over. Didn't you get the letter from my solicitors?'

He counted to three, his hands gripping the telephone with such intensity that he thought he might break it. 'How's Emma?' he asked, his voice cold as steel.

'Didn't you hear me?'

'I heard you, Catherine. I asked you how my daughter is.'

'What do you care?'

That hurt. He felt as though she had stabbed him as surely as if she had stuck a sheaf of cold steel right through his heart. He hated her for that. He took a deep breath and willed himself to keep his temper in check. He forced himself with every fibre of his being to remain silent. He was rewarded when a few moments later he heard Catherine let out a breath.

'She's fine,' she said tight-lipped.

Still he remained silent. There was nothing to say. He pictured his daughter with this Ed and felt physical pain.

'Andy, are you still there?'

'Yes, Catherine.'

The tone of his voice must have communicated something to her because when she next spoke her voice wasn't quite so sharp.

'Look, Andy, it won't do any good you coming over here and trying to break the door down. We've got to move on with our lives.'

'Like you have with Ed?' He spoke calmly but he felt far from calm. He heard her suck in her breath.

'I have found someone else, yes. He's . . . well, we're friends.'

'Lovers?'

'That's—'

'Nothing to do with me? It is when it affects my daughter. I want to know what kind of man is sleeping in the room next to her. What sort of man is playing with her, touching her.'

'Andy, please this is—'

'Getting us nowhere?' He heard her sigh heavily.

'The sooner we get this sorted, the sooner we can move on with our lives.'

'I can't move on with mine until I can prove to you and Emma that I did not rape or even sleep with that girl.'

'And you think that will make everything all right?' she snapped. 'It's gone too far for that.'

He took a breath. 'Not for me it hasn't. You're still my wife and Emma's still my daughter.'

'Andy . . .'

He heard the pleading in her voice but he ignored it. 'I'm not going to let another man have Emma. She's all I've got.'

'Andy . . .'

But he rang off.

ELEVEN

Monday

The discovery on Monday afternoon that the water found on Thurlow's boat definitely contained traces of Hypovase clinched it for Uckfield. Melissa Thurlow was to be brought in for questioning. Her fingerprints had also been found on both the water and tablet bottles but as Horton told Uckfield, you would expect them to be on both if she had packed her husband's sailing bag. It certainly wasn't enough to arrest her, but Horton agreed that the letters, and the fact that a car like hers had been seen in the car park on the night Culven was killed, and that she had no alibi, was sufficient to question her.

Horton knew that Uckfield was keen to get the case cleared up before Friday, the day of his promotion board. He wanted it solved himself. He felt a growing sense of urgency. Catherine's call had made him even more acutely aware of the fact that time was running out. He couldn't afford to fail.

He'd spent the previous day working through Culven's case files, in particular the ones that concerned Jarrett and Thurlow. It made interesting reading. The work that Culven had done for Thurlow was pretty routine stuff, employment contracts with, surprisingly, a couple of recent redundancy settlements. Calthorpe hadn't been telling the truth when he said that Thurlow had no financial worries. Time to call the bank and the accountants.

For Jarrett, Culven's work was more complex. There were several acquisitions and property transactions, both UK based and overseas. Sifting through legal jargon had never been his speciality but someone on the economic crime group, which was part of Special Investigations, could help him. Or they might have done but for the fact he'd alert them of his intentions towards Jarrett. He couldn't afford to do that because he didn't know who was protecting Jarrett. He would just have to continue to wade his way through them and make some telephone calls.

Taylor confirmed that Thurlow had been dragged to the tower in a tender. Horton guessed it was the missing one from the *Free Spirit.* He called the marinas and yacht basins in Chichester and Langstone harbours, and spoke to the harbour masters, but neither had any record of the *Free Spirit* mooring up over Friday night, anywhere. That didn't mean she hadn't. As Horton knew it was easy to pick up a buoy in one of the harbours and go unnoticed.

Earlier that morning he'd designated a team to the painstaking business of tracing and contacting all boat owners in the Emsworth Channel and Northney Marina, both of which were within easy reach of Warlingham Tower. Someone might have seen the *Free Spirit* over the weekend. If that didn't yield any results then he'd widen the area to include Sparkes Yacht Harbour where Charles Calthorpe kept his boat.

The discovery of another body had fuelled the excitement in the station, and, when Melissa Thurlow was brought in, Horton could feel it shift up another gear. He took the seat opposite her in the stifling hot interview room. She looked a little nervous but then, he thought, who wouldn't. His eyes flickered across to the solicitor beside her. He was perspiring freely, dressed as if for winter in a dark blue suit. Just looking at him made Horton break out in a sweat.

Uckfield slowly removed his jacket and hung it carefully on the back of the chair as if it was made of such delicate material that it would disintegrate if treated harshly. He lowered himself carefully onto the hard seat opposite the lawyer.

Kate Somerfield stood, her feet firmly planted a little apart, hands clasped behind her back with her back to the closed door. Horton caught her glance but she stared steadily ahead not acknowledging him. He knew it was more than just professionalism that made her react like that. He was aware that she was from the no smoke without fire brigade as far as Lucy Richardson and her claims were concerned.

The poky room was airless and smelt of body odour and disinfectant. It was like sitting inside a tin can, Horton thought. There were no windows but he could hear the hum of the traffic outside and occasionally the sirens of the police cars as they sped out of the station.

His thoughts had taken him through Uckfield's usual routine with the tape. The lawyer introduced himself as Robert Otton. Horton wasn't that impressed with him. He could smell garlic on his breath. Dandruff was scattered on his collar from his rather flat, dark greasy hair and cigarette ash lay on the lapels of his jacket.

Uckfield began quietly. 'Mrs Thurlow, you understand why you are here, don't you?'

Otton interrupted him,' Chief Inspector, you can't possibly believe that Mrs Thurlow had anything to do with either her husband's death or with Mr Culven's.'

Horton watched as the solicitor mopped his brow. Melissa Thurlow looked cool. She was sitting back in her chair, her posture stiff and upright. Her head was slightly bowed staring at her hands in her lap as though she was going to paint them from memory later. She had abandoned her shorts in favour of pale cream, lightweight linen trousers worn with a light green silk blouse. She would have been better off with the duty solicitor, Horton thought. Uckfield would run rings round this one.

'Why did you kill your husband, Mrs Thurlow?' Uckfield said sharply, ignoring Otton's outburst. 'Is it because you didn't like his sexual preferences?'

She started and her eyes flickered up. Horton saw alarm in them.

'You don't have to answer that, Melissa,' Otton declared.

Uckfield again, sharply, 'Did you kill your husband, because you wanted to be free of him to be with your lover?'

Otton opened his mouth but this time Melissa got there first.

'I didn't kill Roger, Chief Inspector.' Her voice held a numb bewilderment. Her eyes met Horton's. She was no longer the aloof slightly contemptuous woman he'd first met but looked vulnerable and confused. If it was an act then it was a damned good one.

She went on, 'I know nothing about those letters. I never wrote them and I wasn't having an affair with Michael Culven, or any other man. I hardly know, *knew* Mr Culven.'

'We've had the handwriting analysed, Mrs Thurlow. It *is* your handwriting.' Uckfield opened a folder in front of him.

'It can't be,' she declared.

Horton watched her as Uckfield spread out the four letters on the table in front of her. They were encased in plastic evidence bags. Her eyes slowly ran over them. When she looked up he saw confusion.

'I didn't write these.'

Horton saw the first signs of doubt creep into Otton's eyes as he too studied the letters.

Uckfield said, 'How long had you and Culven been planning to murder Roger? Three months, six months, a month? The fog must have been a blessing. Did it hasten your plans?'

'I don't know what you're talking about.' She appealed directly to Horton, who kept his face devoid of any expression.

If he were a betting man he'd say she was telling the truth. There was no other evidence to connect her to Culven. Their questioning of Culven's neighbours had produced no sightings of a woman and there was not a single fingerprint of Melissa Thurlow's in Culven's house, or on these letters.

Uckfield was pressing on. 'You and Culven plotted to kill your husband and when Culven had carried out your wishes, you killed him. You had no further use for him. All you wanted was to be free of your husband.'

Melissa shook her head frowning. 'I can't believe this. It's all utter nonsense, I keep telling you.'

'No. I'll tell you.' Uckfield leaned forward across the desk and Melissa instinctively recoiled. 'You met Culven at Horsea Marina on Friday night. Either you, or Culven, then suffocated Roger, while he was under the influence of the drug, Hypovase, which you put into his bottled water.'

She paled, but with shock or fear? Horton wondered.

Uckfield continued, 'Culven then took the *Free Spirit* through the lock while it was on free flow so that no one would see him. It was foggy so there was hardly anyone about anyway, and he motored down the Emsworth Channel to Warlingham where he put your husband's body in the tender kept on board and then took him ashore in it. He dragged Roger up to the tower and dumped him. He then took the *Free Spirit* back to a nearby mooring and came ashore where you met him, by car, and you spent the night together.'

She was shaking her head looking wretched. Horton thought Otton looked as though he was about to have a heart attack. Every now and then, as Uckfield had ran through his story in a matter of fact voice, Otton had opened and closed his mouth like a fish, but no sound had come from it.

Uckfield leaned back in his seat; he clasped his hands behind his head and went on in a conversational tone. 'On the following Tuesday you called Culven using your husband's mobile phone. We've checked the records. You arranged to meet him on the beach at Eastney. Once there you walked along it together and when Culven's back was turned you strangled him. What did you use? Couldn't have been easy, although Culven didn't look a strong man. Then to slow things down for us you cold-bloodedly bashed his face in.'

'No!' she shouted explosively.

Uckfield ignored her. He leaned back across the table and said softly, 'You have no alibi for Tuesday night and a car, your car, was seen parked.'

'This is preposterous!' exploded Otton. 'What evidence do you have?'

Not enough, Horton knew. He kept his eyes on Melissa.

Uckfield ignored the lawyer. 'We know why you killed your husband, Melissa. Can't say I blame you in a way, a man with perversions like that.'

Her body stiffened and she clasped her hands tightly in her lap.

'I know it takes all sorts,' Uckfield continued, 'but not only was your husband a transvestite but he was also into pornography, the kind that would make your eyes water.' Uckfield sneered and almost laughed. 'What did he ask you to do, eh? Had you got fed up with his sexual demands? A jury wouldn't blame you. We'll show them the magazines, the filth that he liked looking at.'

Her eyes flickered to Otton and back to Horton. It was Horton she finally appealed to.

'What's he talking about, Inspector?'

'We found magazines on your husband's boat,' he replied. 'They contain sex scenes including bondage, and those involving both children and animals.'

'I don't believe you!' The colour drained from her face, her body swayed, first forwards and then against Otton, who put out his hands to hold her.

'A glass of water for my client,' Otton barked as Kate slid out of the room after a nod from Uckfield. 'My client needs a break, Chief Inspector. She's in no fit state to answer any further questions.'

Again Uckfield ignored him. 'Is that why you killed him, Melissa, because you found out about him?'

'No, Roger wasn't like that.' Her voice was barely above a whisper. Her face so pale that it was almost transparent.

Uckfield laughed. 'You expect us to believe that!'

She lifted her eyes and her face looked pinched with pain. 'Roger wasn't interested in sex . . .'

She faltered and Horton was left filling in the blanks. He was beginning to see.

She swallowed hard. The door opened and Kate put the water in front of her. Melissa Thurlow was trembling so much that she had to lift the plastic cup with both hands.

Otton said, 'I think that's enough for now.'

Uckfield slammed the table with his hand. 'It is not enough. Enough is when I get to the truth.'

With an effort she appealed to Horton, 'I am telling the truth.'

'I think not.' Uckfield sat back again. 'Why did you drug him?'

Horton didn't think she could go any paler but she did.

Slowly she said, 'I didn't know what the tablets would do.'

Horton thought Otton was going to have a seizure.

'Melissa, please,' Otton begged.

She ignored him. 'I don't know how he got to the tower or why he was dressed the way he was.'

Horton spoke for the first time. 'Why didn't you simply divorce him?'

'You wouldn't understand,' she replied wearily.

Uckfield rose and said dangerously quietly, 'we *understand* that you, along with your lover, plotted and murdered your husband and then you murdered your lover.'

A flash of anger from her now, perhaps one final effort to convince them.

'That's not true. I have to make you understand. After the death of my father I was lonely and upset and Roger was kind. I thought he loved me but he didn't, he just loved my money and the status it brought him.'

Her eyes looked back down the years. In them Horton saw an empty life.

'Roger wanted a wife with class and breeding,' she continued. 'He wanted to climb the social ladder; marriage to me gave him that. Sir Randall Simpson, my father, was very wealthy. But my friends soon got tired of Roger. I used to watch them cringe at his crude jokes and his constant bragging. I saw pity in their eyes. Poor Melissa, she's really got taken in and landed herself with a right one. So I stopped asking my friends round. Soon I didn't have any. I wasn't going to divorce Roger because that way he'd get his hands on my money, or rather my father's money. And if I had got divorced everyone would pity me and if there's one thing I can't stand it's being pitied. So Roger and I came to an arrangement. I would see he had enough money for all the things he wanted, like his boat, if he left me alone.'

Uckfield was staring at her in disbelief. He towered over the interview table. 'So you started an affair with Culven.'

She swivelled her eyes up to him. 'How many times do I have to tell you? There *was* no affair?' It was as if she had used up her last reserves of energy. She fell back in the chair, a dejected figure.

Otton, tight-lipped, said, 'Chief Inspector, my client is exhausted, as you can see. I insist on a break.'

Uckfield ignored him. 'I've applied for a warrant to search your house. We can wait for that or you can help speed things up by giving us permission now.'

'I've got to stay here? What will happen to Bellman? I've left him in the house.'

Horton said, 'We can take care of your dog. Is there anywhere you would like him to go? A friend or neighbour?' She was shaking her head before he had finished speaking.

'Bellman's never been away from me before.'

'Then we'll take him to kennels.'

'Poor Bellman.'

'Interview terminated, 16.05.' Uckfield switched off the tape and plucked his jacket from the back of the chair. Then leaning towards her again he said, 'We know you killed them both.'

Outside Uckfield grinned at Horton. 'Good result.'

'I'm not sure.'

'She did it all right. She admitted it in there. You heard her.'

'You're going to hold her?'

'You bet I am. I could charge her on that confession alone.'

'Thurlow was suffocated, not poisoned.'

'She could have slipped on that boat and put a plastic bag over his head, while he was drugged.'

'But she couldn't have taken the boat out. She knows nothing about sailing.'

'Lover-boy Culven did.'

Yes, Horton thought, he did.

Uckfield said, 'You just get cracking and get me some evidence. A couple of witnesses would be nice.'

And where do you think I'm going to get them from? A hat? Horton fumed as he watched Uckfield stride away a happy man. Everything he had said made sense, so why did it feel so wrong?

'What happened?' asked Cantelli, when Horton returned to the CID office.

'Uckfield's holding her; he thinks she did it.'

'And you don't?'

'She drugged him, but as to the rest, there are too many unanswered questions for me.' He saw Cantelli glance towards the door. They had the office to themselves. By the look in Cantelli's eyes he could see that he had some bad news.

'I think you should see this, Andy.' He pushed the local newspaper across the desk.

The headline ran, 'Popular PR man killed in Devil's Tower' and alongside the photograph of the tower was a picture of Briarly House. But it was the sub heading that horrified Horton. 'Sex cop leads double murder investigation.'

He felt sick. Soon the national media would pick up on the story. This journalist had dredged up everything he could on his past. There was a small paragraph that said he was unavailable for comment, which made it look as though he had something to hide. Of course he was unavailable, he was working!

He closed the newspaper. How could he fight this? Is this what lay ahead of him every time he handled a prominent case? What chance did he have of any judge giving him access to his daughter?

'They'll get tired of it, eventually,' Cantelli said, but Horton knew what the media were like: once they got hold of a good story they wouldn't let it go easily.

'I don't have *eventually*. I might as well be dead if I can't see Emma again. You of all people should know what my daughter means to me.'

Sadly and quietly Cantelli said, 'I do.'

Horton could see that Cantelli was also thinking about his own problems with Ellen. Activity is what they needed. This case needed solving and he had a point to make not only to Uckfield and Superintendent Reine, but also to the media. And that point was that he was a good detective.

He pulled himself up. 'It's no good us moping, Barney, let's get to work. Uckfield's applied for a warrant to search Briarly House but Melissa Thurlow's given her permission for us to go in there.' Then seeing Cantelli's wary look he added, 'It's OK, Barney, we'll collect a dog handler on our way out.'

There was an accident in Redvins village square and Cantelli was diverted around the back of it past the church. Just coming through the lych-gate were three women carrying floral arrangements. One of them was the oh-so-perfect Alison Uckfield. She looked poised, cool and elegant, a definite asset for a detective superintendent, or a chief constable, Horton thought, with some bitterness. He watched her unlock her car and place the floral arrangement on the back seat before Cantelli turned the corner and she disappeared from sight.

As Horton opened the front door of Briarly House he called to Bellman. The dog gave a soft growl and a bark and then recognising Horton's scent came trotting good-naturedly towards him.

'Your mistress has been delayed and you've got to go on a little holiday.' Horton ruffled the dog's head. Bellman thumped his tail. Horton stepped aside and let Dave the Dog, as he was known around the station, take over.

'See what you can find upstairs, Barney. I'll take downstairs.'

Stepping into the lounge he saw, through the window, Bellman jump into the back of the dog handler's van. His mind wandered back to Alison Uckfield. How much had Catherine confided in her? Should he have a word with Alison to see what he could find out about this Ed? Concentrate damn you, concentrate on the case.

He snatched up a photograph on top of an ancient oak bureau and stared at a portly man in his sixties with silver hair and a wide smile. It must be Melissa Thurlow's father, Randall Simpson. On the top of the bureau there were pictures of a younger Melissa with him. He hardly recognised her. As well as being rich she had also been a beauty, quite a catch for Roger Thurlow, as she had said.

He began a search of the bureau, finding the usual household bills and receipts. There was correspondence between Melissa Thurlow and the local fuchsia society. He flicked open her diary. She had put a line through the Friday her husband was killed and written, South West Fuchsia Show, Swindon. That would be easy enough to check out.

He finished his search finding nothing of interest and crossed the room to scan the books in the bookcase beside the fireplace. He could hear Cantelli moving about upstairs. They were mainly gardening books with one or two biographies and some romantic fiction — Melissa Thurlow's escape? The poor woman hadn't had a great deal of love and romance it seemed with Roger.

His eyes alighted on the painting over the fireplace. It was a fairly competent watercolour of Briarly House. The name in the bottom right hand corner gave him the artist, Melissa's father: Randall Simpson.

Some instinct made him reach out and take it down disturbing the fine cobwebs around it and leaving a faded patch of wallpaper behind it. He turned the painting over to see what, if anything, was written on the back. It wasn't very professionally framed, as around each edge was brown sticky tape that was beginning to come away. Stretching across the back was a piece of string knotted at each end in the eyelets and in the middle a square piece of cream card handwritten with 'Briarly House 1956.' He made to return the picture then changed his mind. His fingers picked at the sticky tape, which came away very easily and slowly he peeled it back. It was all that was holding the backing cardboard in place and as it worked loose he could see something sandwiched between it and the painting itself. With a quickening heartbeat he gently prised the paper out. It was cream and quite delicate.

Putting the picture down, he crossed to the bureau where he slowly unfurled the rectangular piece of paper.

'You found something?' Cantelli asked, crossing the room.

'It's a birth certificate. It was taped to the back of that painting.'

'Strange place to keep it.'

'Not so strange when you take a closer look at it. See the column that gives the name of Melissa's father?

'Unknown,' Cantelli read surprised. 'She was adopted.'

'Yes. By Randall Simpson.'

'So?'

'She obviously didn't want her husband to know otherwise why hide it?'

'But how could that make a difference?'

Horton's mind replayed that last interview with her. From what she had said and left unsaid he could imagine what her life with Roger Thurlow must have been like.

'Roger Thurlow would have used this information to humiliate her,' he said. He couldn't help recalling the taunts of the other children at his school: *your mum doesn't love you; she gave you away*. It wasn't strictly true; his mother had deserted him, though it amounted to the same thing. And some of his foster parents had been just as cruel always telling him he should be 'grateful' for being taken in. In this day and age being adopted wasn't anything to be ashamed of, but he knew that you couldn't help how you felt inside.

He said, 'Thurlow had been gradually chipping away at Melissa's self-confidence, making her feel worthless. If he had discovered this little secret he would have taunted her with it. Melissa has admitted drugging her husband by giving him an overdose but she doesn't strike me as a hardened killer. She'd had enough. She just wanted him out of her life.'

'So Uckfield is right? And she also killed Culven?'

'Why aren't her fingerprints and DNA in Culven's house? Why aren't they on those letters? Get a team in here, Barney. See if we can find any evidence that Culven came here, though I think it unlikely.' Horton slipped the birth certificate into an evidence bag. It might have no bearing on the case but it was one of those oddities. He was interested to see what she would have to say about it.

'They had separate bedrooms,' Cantelli said. 'But his room is like a hotel bedroom. There's nothing personal in it. No papers.'

'And there are no papers here belonging to Thurlow either. There might be a safe. I'll get Marsden to ask her.' Horton pulled out his mobile and rang the station.

They continued their search and had almost finished it when Marsden rang back.

'There's no safe,' Horton told Cantelli.

'So where did he keep his cheque book, bank statements, passport?'

'Where indeed? Let's ask her.'

She said she didn't know. 'Or won't say,' Cantelli ventured, later.

‘We need to cherchez la femme.’

‘Or l’uomo.’

‘Judging by the clothes Thurlow was found dressed in, you could very well be right.’

TWELVE

Tuesday

'Mr Calthorpe's at a client meeting,' Mrs Stephens managed to blurt out in between sobs. Clearly she had taken the news of her boss's death badly. Far worse than his wife, Horton thought, as he looked at her red, swollen eyes. She led him into Thurlow's office, Cantelli following behind.

'Is Mr Parnham in?' Horton hoped the office manager and accountant was. There might be additional information he could give them such as answers to the financial health of the business and any redundancies that Culven had advised on, according to the client files.

'I'll tell him you're here.'

Horton threw himself into Thurlow's large black leather swivel chair and gazed around the spacious and immaculately tidy office. Thurlow had been too important to have filing cabinets in here; they were in Mrs Stephens' adjoining one where he could hear her quiet sobbing.

When he had questioned Melissa about the birth certificate, she had been surprised he'd found it, then fearful and finally relieved, as if it had only just dawned on her, he thought, that her husband was no longer around to verbally torment her. Her reasons for hiding it had been as he had suspected.

He recalled their conversation.

'Do you know who your birth father is?'

'No and I don't care,' she had replied fiercely. 'I was illegitimate, as you now know, but when my mother met Randall Simpson and learned from him that he couldn't have children, I was taken from the Barnados home. I was only two years old, so I don't recall anything about my time in the home.'

Lucky you, Horton thought, her words conjuring up unpleasant memories of his time spent in a home.

'Did your mother ever tell you anything about your father?' He couldn't recall his mother speaking of his father.

'Only that he gave her double trouble. When I asked her what she meant she hinted that I hadn't been her only illegitimate child.'

'Older or younger? Brother or sister?'

'I don't know. Could even have been a twin.'

Horton picked up one of the executive toys on Roger Thurlow's desk and turned it over. As the liquid inside ran down he pulled at the desk drawers and began to poke around inside.

Cantelli took the sideboard on the far wall. 'Not much here. Just drink and some glasses.'

'Nothing here either, stationery, the odd letter, nothing important.'

The door opened and a man swept into the room. He reminded Horton of an actor on a gala night; his manner was confident and self-assured. The eyes were intelligent and assessing behind small John Lennon type spectacles. Uckfield would have approved of that suit. Horton recognised Parnham from the photograph on Thurlow's boardroom wall: he was the runner with the medal and the disabled children.

'I'm sorry to have kept you waiting, Inspector. This is dreadful news. I simply can't believe it. Roger dead!'

'Won't you sit down, Mr Parnham?' Horton gestured him into the chair opposite.

He sat. 'How was Roger killed? Oh I've read about it in the local newspaper and the press have been hounding us ever since but no one's told me what actually happened. I've tried calling Mrs Thurlow but there's no answer. Is it true you've taken her in for questioning? One of the reporters told me. You can't honestly think she has anything to do with this dreadful business?'

He removed his glasses and gave them a quick polish before replacing them. The sun glinting off his spectacles made his expression difficult to read.

Horton said, 'When did you last see Mr Thurlow?'

'Friday before last, when he went to his boat.'

'Did he leave the office before you?'

'Yes. He left at about six thirty. I locked up at seven and went straight to the ferry port. I was catching the eight thirty ferry to St Malo. I have a cottage in north Brittany, a beautiful part of the world. It's just outside Cancale, a village famous for its oyster beds much as Emsworth used to be. That's where I live, Emsworth.'

'And you were in France all weekend?'

'Yes. I returned on Wednesday evening.'

'Did you hear from Mr Thurlow at any time over the weekend?'

'No. Mrs Stephens phoned me on the Monday morning when Roger didn't return. She thought he might have taken his boat across to France to meet me. Then she called me again early on Wednesday morning. I told her to call Mrs Thurlow.'

'How did Mr Thurlow seem to you the last time you saw him?'

Parnham hesitated. For the first time in the interview he looked ill at ease. 'He was OK.'

Parnham was keeping something back, that much was clear to Horton but what and why? Perhaps it was out of loyalty to his late boss? He decided not to press it for the moment. 'Mr Parnham, can you think of anyone who would want to harm Roger Thurlow?'

'No, I can't. He was a very popular man, well liked, especially by his clients.'

Horton fell silent. A telephone was ringing along the corridor; he could hear someone's footsteps hurrying past.

Parnham cleared his throat but just as he made to speak, Horton said, 'Can you tell us why, when we found Mr Thurlow, he should be dressed in women's clothes?'

'Ah.' Parnham showed no signs of being shocked.

'You knew about this?'

'About his dressing up, yes. I found some photographs in his desk. It was about three months ago. I was looking for something else. I asked Roger about them. Of course it was none of my business what he got up to in his spare time but I told him he should either keep that sort of thing away from the office, or at least keep his desk locked. I didn't want to know about it, but I suppose he was relieved to have someone to talk to. He couldn't explain why he did it but he said it, er, gave him a kick.'

'He told you this?' Horton asked surprised.

Cantelli's pen hovered over the notebook.

'We didn't labour over it.'

'He was a transsexual?'

'I wouldn't go as far as to say that. I don't think he went out in the clothes, only dressed up in them in private and . . .' Parnham hesitated. Horton waited.

Parnham shrugged. 'Well I suppose you might as well know it all now, Inspector. There seems no point in keeping anything back. He went to parties; you know the sort of thing I'm sure. Apparently these people advertise in magazines. Sex magazines. I also found one of them in Roger's desk.'

Horton knew all right.

Parnham leaned forward, his expression earnest and concerned. 'Now you can see why I had to confront Roger with it. Can you imagine what would have happened if Mary Stephens, or one of the younger members of staff, had found it?'

Horton thought the younger staff would probably have had a good laugh over it. Mrs Stephens he wasn't so sure about.

'Is there anything else that Roger Thurlow told you about these parties, Mr Parnham?' Horton asked hopefully. Uckfield's conviction that he had found the killer had distracted him. This stank of Jarrett and his blasted club.

Parnham's answer disappointed him. 'No.'

'Did Mrs Thurlow know about her husband's predilection for dressing up in women's clothes?'

'I've no idea. I've hardly spoken to her in all the time I've worked here.'

'And that is how long?'

'Two and a half years.'

Parnham looked worried. 'I don't know what our clients will make of this. Can't it be kept quiet?'

'I'm afraid not, sir. It will come out at the inquest.'

Parnham groaned. 'I'd forgotten that. I don't know what this will do to the business.'

Make it all the more successful I shouldn't wonder, Horton thought with cynicism. 'What about Michael Culven? How well did you know him?'

'He was our company solicitor. He was reviewing our employment contracts.'

'Is that why Roger met him in the yacht club on the Friday lunchtime?'

'Possibly, although they often had lunch together.'

After a short pause Horton said, 'Do you know if Michael Culven shared the same interests as Roger Thurlow.'

'The same . . . ? I don't know. I simply don't know. God, what a mess.'

Horton rose and walked slowly to the big arched window. He looked down on the bustling harbour. 'We'll need to have a look through your client files in case anything there can help us.' He froze. No it couldn't be. The past was playing tricks with him, he'd gone mad; he was seeing things. He blinked hard but when he focused his eyes back on the boardwalk she was still there. God, Lucy Richardson was right there, under his very nose. She was sitting as bold as brass drinking from a bottle, smiling and talking to a dark-haired girl. His stomach did a somersault.

'Sergeant, take over.' he swiftly commanded.

He barely registered Cantelli's surprise before he was out of the door. He couldn't get away quick enough. Down those stairs, turn to his right. Would he get there in time? How much did she have in the bottle to drink? His heart was thumping so fast that it was wonder it didn't explode.

He rounded the corner and drew up with a start. No, it couldn't be. It wasn't possible. Please God, how could you do this to me!

He stared at the table where she'd been sitting but instead of the young, blonde, attractive female there was a fat woman and her equally obese husband. He'd got the wrong table, the wrong bar. She *couldn't* have gone. It had taken him about three minutes at the most to reach her. He wanted to race up to the fat couple and shake and scream at them, demanding to know what had they done with Lucy, but he forced himself to calm down. She couldn't have gone far.

Rapidly he scanned the crowd but there was no Lucy. Perhaps she had gone to another bar. Desperately he searched them all, then the shops, but somehow he knew he wouldn't find her. His chance had come and gone, maybe never to return. He swore softly. There was one last place to look. He should have gone there to begin with.

'Inspector Horton, CID,' he announced into the intercom wondering if he'd be admitted. But they had to. There was no legal reason why they shouldn't admit the police.

After a moment the door buzzed and he stepped into Alpha One's brightly lit and very swish reception. A pretty dark-haired girl of about twenty sat behind a low, grey reception desk. She was wearing a crisp white overall and a worried expression on her perfectly made-up face. Horton could tell instantly that she knew about him by the way her green eyes darted nervously about the room.

'Is Mr Jarrett available?' He flashed his ID knowing damn well that if Jarrett were there he wouldn't deign to see him. There was a camera in the far right hand corner pointing directly at him and, he guessed, one behind him above the door, judging by the way the girl's eyes kept flicking beyond him.

'No. Can I take a message?'

You just have, Horton felt like saying.

'Tell him I'd like to talk to him about Michael Culven. Is he a member?'

'Our membership is strictly confidential.'

'I could insist.'

'Don't you need a warrant?' She'd been well trained.

'I'll come back with one, if it makes you happier.'

He saw the relief in her eyes as he turned to leave. He reached the door before pausing and turning back. 'Oh, I nearly forgot, tell Lucy I'm here, will you?'

'I don't know any Lucy.'

'No?' He eyed her steadily. Her eyes dropped and her face flushed. Lucy was there all right.

'I think you'd better—'

'Leave. Thank you for your help.'

He saw the look of alarm on her pretty young face. She was wondering what help she could possibly have given him. Lucy had to be inside. Where else could she have gone?

He made his way back to Thurlow's office wondering where Lucy was living. If he could only find her. Perhaps he could come here every evening and hang around outside Alpha One. It was a thought.

Cantelli looked up as he entered Thurlow's office. Horton could see he was worried. They were alone.

'It's all right, Barney, I haven't gone mad. I saw Lucy Richardson on the boardwalk.'

Cantelli looked at him incredulously.

'By the time I got there she'd gone. She was in Alpha One but the girl on reception denied it.'

'You've been there? Christ, Andy! Jarrett will make sure Reine throws the book at you.'

Horton rounded on him. 'What else am I supposed to do? Don't tell me to leave it. You know I can't, especially after that newspaper article.'

Horton turned his back on Cantelli and stared out of the window, silently counting to five and trying to still his raging temper. Barney was right. This would mean the end of his police career . . . or would it? He wasn't so sure. Slowly another thought dawned on him. He turned back.

'Jarrett knows that if I get kicked out of the police force I'll be even more of a wild card. He won't go blabbing. He tried that once and it didn't work. No, the only way to get me off his back is to get rid of me — period.'

'Andy, this is too dangerous. You'll get killed.'

'Not if I get to Lucy first.'

Cantelli let out a long slow breath. After a moment he said, 'I'll give a copy of Lucy's photograph to my sister, Isabella; if Lucy goes into the café on the seafront Isabella will let me know.'

Horton hadn't expected that. He was torn between needing Cantelli's help and not wanting him to become involved and end up a possible target himself. In the end, seeing the determined look in his sergeant's dark eyes, he knew that even if he refused, Cantelli would go ahead and do it anyway. He smiled his thanks.

Bringing his thoughts back to the case he said, 'Did Parnham have anything else useful to say?'

'He confirmed that the business hadn't been doing too well lately but he has an appointment with the bank manager. He hopes to get a loan. His story about the porn mags fits. Perhaps Thurlow was simply getting them for his own use and not smuggling them in.'

Perhaps, thought Horton, but he didn't believe it. 'Parnham reminds me of someone, an actor, can't place who though.' His telephone rang. It was Marsden. 'You're sure?' Horton said, surprised. He rang off. 'Well that's a turn-up for the books.'

'What is?'

Horton strode to the door and opened it. 'Wait and see,' he said, tauntingly over his shoulder. 'Mrs Stephens, could you spare us a moment?'

She entered looking wary and perched herself on the edge of the seat opposite Horton poised as if for sudden flight. Her small, dark brown eyes were still puffy.

Cantelli pulled up a chair and sat to the right of Horton.

Horton began gently, smiling sympathetically, trying to put her at ease. 'How long have you worked for Roger?'

She stared nervously at them. 'Twenty-two years.'

'That's a long time. You must have seen many changes.'

And she must have changed in that time too he thought, looking at her. In her early fifties she was short, stout, very plain and motherly. He wondered what she had looked like when she had first started working for Thurlow.

She said, 'To begin with it was just Roger and me in a small office in Old Portsmouth but Roger was so clever that the business simply grew and grew and then we moved here, three years ago.' She faltered and blew her nose.

Horton gave her a moment. Then, 'What was Mr Thurlow like as a boss?'

'Wonderful. He was wonderful,' she stammered and stuffed her handkerchief to her mouth to stop herself from crying. 'Not that everyone appreciated his talents.'

'What do you mean?'

'Roger had such high standards that not everyone could meet them. He was very strict with staff, and you know what young people are like today.'

'Was there anyone in particular he upset?'

She looked at him surprised. 'No. Not really.'

Horton let it go for now but a list of staff that had been sacked, or had resigned, over the last year might be helpful. Parnham could give them that. He said, 'I understand this must be very painful for you, Mrs Stephens, but we need all the help we can get to try and find out who killed Roger.'

She turned a sob into a gulp and drew in her breath. Twisting her handkerchief in her podgy hands she stammered, 'I can't believe that someone could do such a dreadful thing.'

'How well do you know Melissa Thurlow?'

She looked surprised and tensed at the sudden change of subject. 'Not that well. She never came to the office.'

'You didn't go to Briarly House?'

'Oh no.'

'Why not?' he asked quietly.

'Mrs Thurlow doesn't like visitors. She's an invalid.'

Horton sensed Cantelli's surprise and stifled his own excitement.

Mrs Stephen's explained, 'She suffers from agoraphobia, you see. That's why she never came to the office, or to any of our functions. Poor Roger.'

Poor bloody Mrs Stephens, Horton thought as Cantelli cleared his throat. Thurlow had spun her a pack of lies for years. He didn't like being the one to disillusion her but if he didn't someone else would and that would probably be the media. Horton knew he was going to be cruel but he had no option. 'I think you'll find that Roger has lied to you, Mrs Stephens.'

Again that shake of her head and the fierce twisting of her handkerchief in her lap. 'He wouldn't.'

'Mrs Thurlow does not suffer from agoraphobia. In fact, she spends most of her time outside the house cultivating fuchsias. She travels the country showing them.'

'I don't believe you. Roger wouldn't . . .' Her voice trailed off as she looked at each of them in turn.

'Why did he feel it necessary to lie to you?' Horton persisted, his voice harsher now.

'I don't know.' But her face was gaining its colour and now she was squirming in her seat.

'I think you do know. Why do husbands lie about their wives? Why would Roger want to impress his secretary, Mrs Stephens?'

She stared at her hands. He felt sorry for her.

'And why,' he added, 'would a man leave his secretary his entire estate?'

Her head shot up and she looked blank in amazement. Genuine? Perhaps, he thought.

'You are named as sole beneficiary in Mr Thurlow's will. Was that for services rendered beyond and above the call of duty as a secretary?' he said, to provoke a response.

She flushed angrily. 'It wasn't like that. You don't understand. How can any of you understand? I loved Roger.'

Relentlessly Horton pursued his course. 'And I suppose he told you he loved you?'

'He did.' She stared at him with hatred. 'He *did* love me. He loved us both.'

'Both?'

'Me and Susan. My daughter. Our daughter.'

THIRTEEN

Wednesday

'We found Roger Thurlow's cheque books, passport and financial papers at Mary Stephens's flat in Western Parade,' Cantelli said at the briefing the following morning. 'He'd been dividing his time between there and Briarly House for years.'

'But not his affections according to Melissa Thurlow,' Uckfield said.

Horton shifted position. The incident room was unbearably hot. Two large fans whirred in opposite corners and every now and then as they swept the room they lifted the papers on the desk like a sigh.

Horton said, 'Roger liked the best of both worlds, Melissa and Briarly House for money and status, and Mary Stephens for sex and comfort.'

'Where's the daughter?' asked Uckfield.

'Travelling Australia,' Cantelli said. 'We've checked she is there.'

'Does she know about her father's death?'

'She does now. We let her mother break the news to her first.'

Horton thought that Cantelli looked haggard. He'd heard him earlier on the telephone to Charlotte. Whatever Charlotte had told him it hadn't helped. Horton had spent a restless night himself; churning over the case and the fact that Lucy was back in town. After his visit to Alpha One he'd been half expecting something to happen but he'd arrived at his boat without any mishap.

Horton said, 'He's given her a good education and not seen her go without.'

'So not a complete bastard,' Uckfield muttered, turning towards the fan.

'Rather arrogant was how some of the staff described him,' Cantelli chipped in. 'Flashy and mean were the other two words that kept cropping up.'

Yesterday afternoon and again this morning a team were in Thurlow's taking statements and going through the files.

'How deeply in debt was he?' Uckfield asked.

Marsden piped up. 'There's a mortgage on Mrs Stephens' flat and a marine mortgage on the boat. Briarly House is in Mrs Thurlow's name and there's no mortgage. The directors have been taking substantial dividends from the company over the last four years and it went into loss last year for the first time. Once Roger Thurlow's debts are paid off I don't think Mrs Stephens will get much, although there is some life insurance.'

'Enough to kill for?' asked Uckfield.

Horton said, 'Not really. Mary Stephens has an alibi for the time of both murders. A friend stayed with her on the Friday night of Thurlow's death and on the night Culven was killed she was at a pottery evening class and went for a drink with a friend after it. She worshipped the ground Thurlow walked on.'

'Which is more than his wife did.'

Horton knew the meaning behind Uckfield's comment. He said, 'There is no sign of Culven's fingerprints in Briarly House. If he and Melissa were having an affair then they didn't conduct it in either of their homes. We're still looking for the tender from the *Free Spirit* and Culven's Mercedes, but Thurlow's car has been found abandoned on Paulsgrove estate.'

Walters said, 'Melissa Thurlow's alibi partly checks out. She was at the South West Fuchsia Show in Swindon on Friday but she didn't stay overnight. She left at eight thirty p.m.'

Uckfield said, 'Time enough to get back and collect her lover after he had disposed of Thurlow's body.'

The briefing ended. Uckfield stormed out. Horton followed. He could see that the pressure was getting to the DCI. He didn't blame him. This was one of those frustrating cases.

'Are you going to release Melissa Thurlow?' he asked. The thirty-six hours was up at 11 a.m. this morning, after that Uckfield would have to take the case before the magistrates' court who could authorise further detention for up to ninety-six hours. 'I'm still not convinced she's our murderer, Steve.'

Uckfield stopped. He turned and began to count off on his fingers. 'One, she has motive, especially if she knew about Mary Stephens; two, she has no alibi for the time of either deaths; three, she has confessed to drugging her husband; four she was having an affair with Culven, the handwriting on the letters check out, and five a car like hers was seen on the promenade the night Culven was killed. In my book that adds up to a satisfying arrest, certainly enough for me to take it to the magistrates' court.'

Horton could see there was no shifting Uckfield from that view, and he did have a point, several in fact. He could charge Melissa for the murder of her husband but Culven?

'It's all a bit circumstantial. I can't see the CPS going for it.'

'Then you'd better pull your finger out, Inspector and get me some evidence.' Uckfield glared at him.

'And where does the great man suggest we get it from?' Cantelli said, after Horton had relayed an edited version of the conversation to him.

'We're missing something, Barney.' Maybe if he confided his theories about Jarrett to Uckfield they might be able to fill in some of the pieces, or at least legitimately question the man. But Horton wasn't yet ready to tell Uckfield. 'Let's assume that Melissa is telling the truth, even about those letters.' Horton pushed away a pile of papers on Cantelli's untidy desk. 'We'll also assume that Roger Thurlow was the intended victim and that Culven's death was secondary. Culven was laid out like a crucifix to make a point. He was killed as some kind of sacrifice.'

'For what?'

'To frame Melissa, just as those letters were forged, to point the finger at her.'

'Why?'

'Jealousy?'

'Mary Stephens wasn't jealous of Melissa: the poor cow pitied her. Someone from the fuchsia club?'

Despite his weariness Horton smiled. 'I can't see anyone going to those lengths just because she pipped them to first prize.'

His eyes flickered to the wall behind Cantelli. Pinned on his notice board were photographs of his five children with Charlotte; they were all smiling. The twins had drawn Cantelli a picture each: Joe a fire engine and Molly a house, and they had written their names carefully underneath their artistic endeavours. Where were all the pictures Emma had drawn for him? He'd left the house in a hurry and didn't even have one. Did she still draw them for him and did Catherine rip them up? Or had Catherine told her that nasty daddy didn't deserve to have any pictures?

Cantelli broke through his thoughts. 'Why would someone be jealous of Melissa Thurlow? Ok so she's got a nice house and loads of money, not that you'd think it looking at the state of Briarly House, but Marsden's checked out her bank and savings account and she's rolling in it.'

'Which she inherited from her adoptive father.' Horton suddenly felt better as his ideas crystallised. The weariness sloughed off him. 'That's it Barney. It has to be. Someone is jealous of her inheriting his fortune. I want Randall Simpson's background checked out. I want to know everything about him and his relatives. Is there someone out there who doesn't think she should have inherited all of Simpson's wealth?'

'If there is he's taken a long time to get even; must be a very patient man.'

'What was it John Dryden said? Beware the fury of the patient man.'

'Was Dryden a cop then?'

Horton smiled. 'No an English poet and playwright. He was England's first Poet Laureate in 1668.'

'I'm impressed. I never knew you had such a good education.'

'I didn't. Not at the Sir Wilberforce Cutler Comprehensive, no one did, but my last foster mother, Eileen, was a very educated woman and loved poetry, some of it rubbed off on me.'

'So why didn't this man try to get even with Melissa before now?'

'Perhaps he's been abroad and has just found out she inherited a pile. Or he might have been ill, in hospital or in prison. He wants revenge for Melissa stealing what he thinks should have been his.'

'Randall Simpson couldn't have any children.'

'There might be a brother, sister, cousin, great aunt. See if you can find any relatives, Barney. It won't be too difficult; he was a prominent businessman. Meanwhile I'm going to have a word with Melissa.'

There was hope in her eyes when she entered the interview room, which Horton had to quickly dash by telling her that it was likely she would be detained for further questioning.

'You can't still think I killed Roger and Michael!'

'I'd like to ask you some questions about Randall Simpson. Do you want your lawyer present?'

She looked surprised then with a wave of her arm and irritation on her tired face said, 'No.'

'Did he have any relatives?'

'No.'

'None?'

'I don't know what Randall has to do with all this, Inspector, but if you really must know he was an orphan. He was brought up in a Barnardo's Home.'

Dead end then? No, not yet. There must be someone. But then he had no one, except Emma, his daughter, and he was terrified of losing her. 'Did he ever try to trace his family?'

'He might have done. He never said.'

'What about his birth certificate? Do you have a copy?'

'It's in a tin in my wardrobe.'

'Can you remember what's on it?' They'd check anyway.

'You mean his mother and father's name? There's nothing or rather it says "unknown". He was found abandoned outside a hospital in Guildford in 1908.'

This wasn't going to be easy, Horton thought, with annoyance. But someone must have traced Randall's past. Someone who had good cause to think they should have been entitled to Randall's fortune.

'Have you ever been approached by anyone claiming to be a relative of Randall?'

She looked surprised. 'No. Why this interest, Inspector?'

'I think it's possible someone might have framed you.'

'Then you believe I'm innocent?' Her face brightened.

'Has there ever been anyone enquiring about your late father's background?'

She ran a hand through her hair and thought for a moment. Then he saw her eyes light up. She sat forward with a faint flush on her face. 'Of course, how could I have forgotten? There was someone. He was writing a book about Randall, a biography. He examined my father's papers and asked me questions.'

'Who was he?' Horton asked eagerly.

She frowned. 'I can't recall his name.'

'No matter we can look it up. Did he give you a copy of the book?' Horton didn't remember seeing one in the bookshelves.

'No.' She looked puzzled. 'I'd forgotten all about it. It must be at least eight years ago.'

'Can you describe him?'

She let out a breath, shaking her head. 'He was sort of ordinary.' She closed her eyes for a moment trying to visualise him. Horton silently urged her to remember something, anything. After a moment she said, 'He was about my age, possibly a bit younger, like I said just ordinary. I *am* sorry, Inspector. Perhaps if I'd had a copy of the book I might have remembered him but when he didn't send me one and I didn't hear from him again I just assumed he hadn't bothered to write it.'

'You didn't check to see if it had been published?'

'No.'

He thought that a little odd.

She said, as if interpreting his silence, 'If it had been published Roger would have told me. He would have capitalised on it.'

'And that's why you never mentioned it to him?'

'I thought if it comes to something then so be it. But I hoped it wouldn't. Every time there was an article in the newspapers or magazines about Randall, Roger would call the journalists and try and get some publicity for himself out of it.'

And you just wanted to be left alone with your memories and your fuchsias, Horton thought. He told her that if anything else occurred to her to let the custody clerk know. He relayed the information to Cantelli, instigated the search for the book and the biographer, whom he believed was bogus, and sent Marsden out to collect Randall Simpson's birth certificate from Briarly House.

It was just after five when Cantelli put his head round the door of his office. 'You hungry?'

'No. I'm hot, tired, irritated, dirty and frustrated. I know I'm right, Barney, but who is this biographer?'

'What you need is a nice cup of tea and a breath of fresh sea air. I know just the place.'

It took a moment for Horton to follow Cantelli's train of thought. When it clicked he felt a shiver of anticipation that quickened his pulse and set the hairs pricking at the back of his neck. He hardly dared to hope. 'Isabella's seen Lucy?'

'And there's more. She knows where Lucy lives.'

The journey from the station to the seafront seemed to take forever. Horton could barely conceal his impatience. He couldn't speak. He didn't even want to think. He'd had too many hopes dashed to raise them too high. Perhaps Isabella was mistaken and the girl she had discovered was some other blonde? Please God, let it be her. Just the chance to talk to her once that was all he asked. It wasn't much, surely?

Isabella Cantelli greeted them warmly as they stepped into the seafront café, a smile lighting her dark, finely-boned face.

'I didn't expect to find you behind the counter,' Cantelli addressed his sister.

'Short staffed. Either I muck in or we lose custom. Let me get you a drink and then I'll get Adrienne to cover for me.'

Cantelli ordered his usual double espresso. Horton didn't want a drink, he wanted Lucy's address but he could hardly blurt that out. Curbing his impatience with great difficulty he ordered a coffee and stared at the colourful and numerous handwritten signs stuck in a seemingly haphazard manner on the wall behind Isabella, offering him amongst many other things the choice of an all-day breakfast, sausage and chips, toasted teacake and coffee special. He watched Isabella as the coffee machine went through its noisy routine to the accompaniment of the burbling DJ on the local radio station, praying she hadn't got this wrong. Hoping that this wasn't a wild goose chase.

Finally, after what seemed like an eternity to Horton, they took their drinks to one of the aluminium tables. The café was deserted inside but outside, the veranda, which gave on to the beach, was crowded.

A minute later Isabella joined them. She sat down opposite Horton and leaning forward said quietly, 'She came into the café today. She'd been on the beach and wanted a drink. She's a pretty girl and bright too, I'd say.'

Horton felt stifling hot. His hands were sweating. His heart was beating rapidly.

'I recognised her immediately from the photograph in the paper that Barney gave me. I got talking to her. It's easy when you're pouring someone a drink, or wiping down their table. She was with another girl, dark-haired, surly looking.'

'That's the one she was with at Oyster Quays,' Horton interjected, his voice strained with tension.

'I know where she lives. Well, I know the road and I know what the house looks like, so the rest is up to you, detective. It's a three-storey house in St Ronald's Road. There aren't that many because the road was bombed in the war and rebuilt afterwards. We had an aunty who lived there.' She flashed a look at Cantelli. 'Lucy's got a flat or bed-sit there.'

To Cantelli, Horton said. 'I need to follow this up.'

'For God's sake be careful, Andy.'

With a promise that he would, he went in search of St Ronald's Road. It was a long road, with a big church on the corner. It curved in the middle and came out by a small park at the opposite end. It had taken him five minutes to walk there. This was, as Isabella had said, bed-sit land. The houses were shabby, smelly and occupied by students, benefit claimants and asylum seekers.

It didn't take Horton long to find Lucy's flat. There were only five three-storey houses in the road. He came across Lucy's name on a piece of paper roughly jammed into a pigeonhole used for post in the grimy hall. Climbing the stairs in the dilapidated and dirty Edwardian house, with his heart pounding and his mouth dry, he found flat three and knocked on the door. There was no sound from inside. He knocked again. Still nothing. After a while he crossed to the flat opposite where he could hear music playing and knocked. A girl with greasy black hair and a nose stud eventually answered and eyed him with hostility.

'No need to break the bloody door down. What do you want?'

'Do you know where Lucy is?'

'Who wants her?'

'I do.'

'And who the fuck are you?'

'Do you know where she is?' he repeated tersely.

'No. But I'm free if you're not doing anything.' She leered at him and stood provocatively with her hands on her hips.

'No, thanks.'

'Please yourself.' She slammed the door on him.

Slowly he made his way down the stairs feeling deflated but told himself that at least now he knew where to find her. It was only a matter of waiting until she showed up. He took up position on the corner of a small cul-de-sac almost opposite. Slowly the mist began to roll in. People returned to their homes, lights came on and the air became clammy and chilly. Various people went in and out of number fourteen but Lucy wasn't one of them.

He pulled up the collar of his jacket and dashed a glance at his watch. He hesitated wondering whether to break into her flat and wait for her there, but that would only give her cause to complain, and perhaps worse, make up some other cock and bull story about him molesting her. No, better to wait outside and catch her before she went in. He was hungry and thirsty but his throat was so tight and his stomach was so tense that he doubted he would be able to get anything down. Still no sign of Lucy. Where the hell was she? Just his luck that she'd choose to spend this night out on the town or with that friend of hers.

He waited until midnight feeling damp, cold, disappointed and irritated and then headed back to his boat. Was nothing ever going to be easy for him? All he wanted was one tiny little break but it seemed he was going to be denied even that.

He lay on his berth, the hatch slightly open, listening to the foghorns, determined that he wouldn't sleep but eventually fatigue overcame frustration and he drifted off.

He awoke suddenly and lay perfectly still. Something had jolted him out of a dream filled sleep — a sudden movement or noise. He was wide-awake now filled with a sense of danger that was so strong it chilled the blood in his veins. Yes, he could hear footsteps.

He swung his legs over the bunk and strained his ears. The footsteps were directly outside his boat. Horton sensed rather than saw someone crouching. Then the sound of something being unscrewed. He felt the boat move, but not as though someone was climbing on board; someone was loosening his stern line. The footsteps came again, padding softly on the wooden pontoon. Now he was aft. Yes, the line was definitely being loosened. There was only one line left now holding amidships.

With his body racing with adrenalin he slid off his bunk, crouching low. He could hear the sound of liquid being poured and then that smell. He couldn't mistake it. The bastard. He had but a second to get out before the match was struck and his boat would go up like a firework. There was only one way to do this and that was to startle the man before he could strike that match.

Mustering all his power he roared, 'Go!' leapt over the washboard and was on the black hooded figure, knocking the can from his hand on to the pontoon and the unstruck matches with it. The intruder recovered with surprising agility. He swung round and was running up the pontoon. Horton set off after him, his bare feet striking against the wood. The figure picked up a set of wooden steps that led up to a large motorboat and threw them at him. Horton dodged, but lost his foothold and stumbled. It gave the intruder just enough time to punch the security release on the gate and leap up the jetty, where a car was revved up and waiting. Before Horton could reach it the car was squealing and screeching out of the marina.

Eddie came charging out. 'What's happened?'

'Someone tried to break into my boat,' he panted.

'You all right?'

'Yes.' But it had been a very close call.

'Do you want me to phone for the police?'

'I am the police.'

'Yeah, sorry, I forgot.'

Whoever it was would be back, of that Horton was sure.

'Someone after you?'

'You could say that.' Horton replied with feeling. Then seeing Eddie's worried expression added, 'It's OK. I'll move her for a while.'

'Whatever you say, Andy.'

Horton couldn't mistake his relief. Eddie didn't want a burning boat, or several boats if the fire spread, on his hands. And Horton was certain that whoever it was would try again.

He returned to his boat and sniffed the air. There was the distinct smell of petrol but thankfully he had stopped the intruder before he could splash it around too much. With the boat partly made of wood and the petrol already in the outboard engine, it would have gone sky high if a sixth sense, a premonition, call it what you will, hadn't alerted him.

It was foggy and close on three o'clock but that couldn't be helped. Slowly and thoroughly he began to wash down the boat, as his mind turned over the possible identity of his attacker. Try as he might he couldn't recognise him. He hadn't had a chance to see his face in the dark, and cloaked as it was. Why try to fry him alive? But he knew the answer to that question. The intention had clearly been to kill him. He needed to be silenced. And silenced before he could speak to Lucy. Someone had seen him outside Lucy's flat.

FOURTEEN

Thursday

'Where's Cantelli?' Horton asked, trying to hide his annoyance that it was Walters who was collecting him from the Hayling Ferry, Portsmouth side and not the sergeant.

'Problems at home,' Walters said, almost with relish.

Damn, he had been planning on Cantelli dropping him off outside Lucy's flat, but now he'd have to postpone his visit. He couldn't ask Walters to take him there, because he'd go running back to Uckfield.

Walters sneezed out of the car window and Horton was glad he'd remembered to let it down. He would collect his Harley from the station and bike back to Southsea as soon as Walters dropped him off. He dashed a glance at his watch. It was early yet just after nine. Lucy was probably still in bed, but whose? Had she eventually returned home?

For the first time in a week there was no sign of fog. The day had dawned sticky hot and humid. There seemed to be no air and the heavy blue grey sky was pressing down on them.

'Culven's Mercedes has been found.'

'Where?' Horton was torn between excitement at the news and frustration that it would delay him seeing Lucy.

'Stansted Woods.'

Not far from Briarly House and just one more factor that helped to point towards Melissa.

'There's not much of it left; it's been flashed up.'

'Not much point in going out there then. Leave it to the forensic team and head for the station. Anything more on Randall Simpson's past?'

'Not a dickie bird and there's no sign of this biography either. I reckon it was just a con.'

Horton did too. He opened his window to try and catch some breeze and dispel the body odour that was emanating from Walters. He also hoped it would help keep him awake. He hadn't slept apart from that first hour or so before his intruder had tried to roast him. He rested his arm on the windowsill wondering about Cantelli and his problems — must be Ellen. He hoped it wasn't too serious.

His mind turned, as it had most of the night, to his attacker. He had been too tall for Jarrett. The only conclusion he could draw was it must be one of Jarrett's employees.

The radio crackled into life. It was Trueman.

'I don't think you're going to like this much, Andy,' he began warily. 'We've had a report of a woman found dead at Southsea in suspicious circumstances.'

Why did Horton's mind leap to Lucy Richardson? Was it the way Trueman had spoken and his words? Or was it because someone had tried to silence him last night and they might have tried and succeeded with Lucy.

'Where?' he asked, hoping he was wrong. Lots of women lived in Southsea. But he had been watching and waiting for one there last night before the attempt on his life.

'Fourteen St Ronald's Road.'

Horton's heart sank. It was Lucy's address but maybe not her flat but he knew it had to be.

'Have we got an ID?' he asked almost reluctantly.

'Yes.

'It's alright Dave you don't need to tell me, I can hear it in your voice. It's Lucy Richardson, isn't it?

'It appears so.'

Trueman said something about the DCI but Horton had stopped listening. He gave instructions to Walters to head for St Ronald's Road. Walters gave him a look that said, on your head be it, before dodging into a side street of terraced houses, which would take them back to Southsea. Uniform had the area cordoned off when they arrived and a small crowd had already gathered. Walters parked in the middle of the road and a constable lifted the tape, which they ducked under before heading up the steps through the open door and into number fourteen.

Horton climbed the stairs, his tread as heavy as his heart with the thought of Lucy's death along with the fact that he might never get to the truth of why she had lied, who had told her to and why he therefore might never clear his name and restore his reputation. With Walters trailing behind him, he steeled himself for what he was going to see.

'Who found her?' he asked, pausing in the doorway. Her naked body was sprawled on the bed. Her eyes were open. Her long blonde hair was spread out on the bed behind her; he could see its dark roots. Her throat was livid with the marks of strangulation.

Marsden was watching him carefully from the far side of Lucy's bed. His back was to the window, which led out on to a fire escape; his fair, angular face was pale. He looked a little shaken and also a little afraid of him, Horton thought.

'Jane Staveley; she's waiting in the flat next door,' Marsden replied. 'She ran there as soon as she discovered the body. The flat belongs to a man called Simon Howgate. I think he's Jane's boyfriend but she says she doesn't live there with him. He left before we showed up. Do you think I ought to put a call out for him, sir?'

'Let's get some facts first.' Behind him he could hear Walters' laboured breathing. 'Who's with Jane Staveley now?' He wondered if his voice sounded as tense as he felt.

'Somerfield.'

He should have prevented this. Had Lucy already been dead last night when he had knocked on her door? If so, then the girl opposite could give a description of him. Had the attempt on his life been designed to stop him getting to Lucy before she could be silenced forever?

Now that his first sense of shock and outrage was beginning to ease, he felt pity for her. She looked so young, so innocent, even though he knew she wasn't the latter. For the first time he wondered who her parents were. Where had she come from? What was her background?

He peeled his eyes away from the bed and gazed around the pathetic little room: the dirty curtains hanging limp in the sun; the smell of months — no years — of dust and fluff accumulating in corners and under the sagging, stained mattress; the threadbare square of a once red carpet that didn't reach the walls with dirty linoleum protruding from it, and the shabby, second-hand furniture probably picked up in cheap fly-by-night shops in the seedier parts of town; it still smelt of the old dead people whose houses it had come from.

He said, 'I'll talk to Jane Staveley. Let me know when the doctor arrives.'

Jane Staveley was the girl he'd seen with Lucy at Oyster Quays. Her very short skirt showed off well-shaped calves and over-large thighs. A skimpy top had slipped off her narrow hunched shoulders displaying a large tattoo in the shape of a flower on her right shoulder. She didn't look any more than twenty. Her mascara had run where she had been crying and she sniffed into a sodden tissue. He saw hostility in her muddy brown eyes as he entered.

He began gently. 'Jane, I know this must be very upsetting for you, but do you think you could tell me what happened?'

He perched on the unmade bed beside her. The duvet cover had been thrown back, revealing a dark blue polyester sheet that didn't look too clean. This room was a replica of Lucy's with its cheap furniture and soiled curtains. In the left-hand corner was a small sink, cooker and fridge, while opposite in the far right hand corner was a large and very expensive hi-fi system. Clothes were scattered all over the floor along with unwashed plates, mugs, and takeaway foil containers, some of which still had the remains of curry and Chinese food in them. The window was shut and the smell of the shabby bed sitting room clawed at Horton's throat making him want to retch. He didn't blame Kate Somerfield for hovering in the open doorway.

Jane took a deep breath. 'We were going to the beach. When she didn't show by the pier like we'd arranged I came to see why. I thought she might have changed her mind and gone out with her flash boyfriend.'

'His name?'

Jane brushed her limp hair off her face. Her gold bangles jangled noisily. 'I don't know; I never saw him and she wouldn't say. She just told me he had loads of money and was dead posh.'

'Did she describe him at all?' It couldn't be Jarrett, could it? He had money but Horton wouldn't describe him as posh.

Jane shook her head. 'No. She had a date with him last night.'

'When did she first meet him?'

'About a week ago, I think, soon after . . .'

'After what?'

But Jane had clammed up. She pressed her lips together, put the tissue to her mouth and glared at him defiantly.

'When did Lucy come back to Portsmouth?' he asked casually, although he felt far from casual.

'Two weeks ago. Why?'

'How did you get into Lucy's flat?'

'I've got a key.'

'And when you went in you found her exactly as she is? You didn't touch anything?'

'No. I called you lot straightaway,' she gulped. He was glad she had. Girls like Lucy and Jane usually didn't. Tears looked set to spill again only she sought refuge in her anger. 'I hope you get the bastard who did this to Lucy and lock him up for good.'

Some hope, Horton thought cynically. Oh, they might get him but he doubted if he'd be locked up for good. Someone knocked lightly on the door, and he saw Somerfield dealing with it. 'Have you any idea who might have done this to her, Jane?'

'Some weirdo.'

'Inspector Horton, the doctor's just arrived and the DCI's on his way,' Kate Somerfield said.

'Horton! You're Horton?' Jane asked sharply, widening her eyes.

'Yes, why?' He tried to sound calm but his insides were churning. Clearly Lucy had told Jane about him. He sensed Somerfield's quickening interest and looked up to see her face impassive but her eyes full of curiosity. With a pointed glance at her, Jane pressed her lips together. Horton got the message.

'Leave us for a moment, Somerfield,' he commanded. She went, but he could see it was reluctantly.

The room was stifling hot and the smell was making him feel nauseous. He wanted to throw open the windows but he forced himself to sit beside Jane and look at her with as neutral an expression as possible. Slowly and evenly he said, 'Jane, this is important. Did Lucy tell you about me?'

She nodded. 'She said you were nice and very dishy and she was right.'

'What did she say?' Horton ignored the compliment and the leer that went with it.

'That this bloke approached her and asked her if she'd like to earn a few extra bob. All she had to do was get you into a hotel bedroom and say you raped her, or slept with her or something, anything to get you away from there.'

'Away from where?' he asked evenly, though his heart was racing. He wanted to hear her say it. He could hardly breathe. His body was tense in anticipation of her answer. He'd waited eight months for this. Christ! If only Catherine were here now?

'That posh gym. Alpha One.'

And there it was; said so simply that he was almost afraid he hadn't heard correctly. '*When* was she told to do this?' Had it been before he'd accidentally met her or while he was wining and dining her?

'How should I know?' Jane said surprised.

'Who paid her?'

Jane shrugged her tattooed shoulder. 'Don't know. Honest I don't. She wouldn't tell me; afraid that I might muscle in on her little game.'

Horton looked quizzically at her. He understood her meaning but wanted her to say it.

'That's why she came back to Portsmouth,' Jane continued. 'She wanted more money and said she could get it easily.'

'She was blackmailing someone?'

Jane sniffed. 'I don't know as I'd call it that.'

'Then what would you call it?' Horton said scathingly, but it was wasted on her.

'Just a way of earning money.'

'Who was she blackmailing, Jane?' he asked eagerly.

'I don't know. She just said he would pay quite a lot for his little secret not to come out.'

'What secret?' He was getting there. At last!

'If I knew that, I might have a chance of earning a bit of extra money on the side,' Jane said tartly.

'I thought you didn't know who her victim was.'

'I don't but I could put two and two together and—'

'End up like Lucy,' snapped Horton.

Jane writhed. 'Yeah, well, I don't know. All I know is he's someone quite high up.'

Horton quickly picked up on this. It was as he had suspected. He hadn't been imagining it. 'In the police force, you mean?'

'She didn't say that, just said someone important like.' But Jane's dark face had flushed betraying her. That ruled out Dennings, Horton thought, but it still left Reine and his ex-boss, Underwood.

'Who was he, Jane?' he asked again.

'I honestly don't know.'

He held her gaze but could see that she was telling the truth. Lucy had guarded her secret and her income well. 'Did Lucy ever say why she was told to lie?'

'No.'

And now she was dead. 'And what about you? Have you ever worked for Alpha One?'

'Me? No.' Her answer didn't quite have the ring of truth about it. She looked away and began shredding her tissue.

'Are you sure, Jane? '

'Of course I'm sure.' She wouldn't look at him.

'It might help us to find Lucy's killer if you were to tell the truth.'

He left a silence and in the end she was forced to say, 'All right then but I didn't work for them, Lucy arranged it.'

'Arranged what?'

'Lucy and me, we were in that tower, the one where the body was found.'

'When?' he asked keenly.

'Friday night, just a week ago.'

The night Thurlow was dumped there. 'Why were you there?'

'It was a party.'

'Arranged through Alpha One?'

'Lucy said it would be all right and we'd get well paid. She'd done this sort of thing before, loads of times.'

'What sort of thing?' He could feel his heart knocking against his rib cage. He knew the answer.

'Escorts, that kind of thing.'

'Who were you with, Jane?'

'I don't know their names; it was just a couple of blokes. They were into black magic, devil worship, bondage, that sort of stuff, and in that hole.' She shuddered. 'It gave me and Lucy the creeps.'

'How many of them were there?'

'Two.'

'What time did you get there?'

'About midnight. We were only there for about an hour. We were told it was a birthday surprise.' She sniffed and the tears filled her eyes once again as she remembered her friend was dead.

'And you didn't see the body in the tower?'

She widened her eyes at him. 'Are you kidding?' She suddenly stopped, her face blanched and her hand shook.

'What is it, Jane? You've remembered something?'

She gulped and nodded. 'I'd forgotten. Lucy went back. She'd lost her lighter.' Horton wouldn't mind betting that was the lighter he'd found on his boat. 'We'd got halfway down that track, you know the one from the tower, when she grabbed my arm and said she had to go back.'

'You didn't go back with her?'

'No way. That place gave me the creeps. I walked to the road and hitched a lift back to Portsmouth. Was lucky to get one, until the pervert who picked me up fancied his chances.'

'What was his name?'

'How the hell do I know, I didn't ask.'

'What was he like? What car did he drive?'

'Flashy BMW. He was about forty, fat, and stunk of booze. It was hardly worth the bother really but he seemed satisfied.'

'And what about Lucy? What happened to her?'

'Not much. She got back all right. I didn't ask how.'

So Lucy could have seen the body being dumped after the others had left. The killer, fearing that she had seen him, had silenced her. But it had taken him eleven days to do so. Why wait that long? Perhaps he was Lucy's new boyfriend. So was Jarrett off the hook over Lucy's death? It buggered up his theory of Jarrett silencing Lucy before he could speak with her. His mind was still as full of questions as it was empty of answers.

'Have you any idea who the men in the tower were? It's important Jane.'

After a moment's hesitation she said, 'I know one of them was a dentist. He was joking about his clients. He was into bondage. The other one was a solicitor. He liked being beaten with a cane, sad bastard.'

And that, thought Horton, described Michael Culven exactly.

FIFTEEN

'Dr Price thinks she's been dead about fourteen to sixteen hours,' Horton told Uckfield, as they stepped outside. An officer catalogued their departure from the house and Horton nodded at the photographer as he entered. 'That would make it between six and eight o'clock last night.' While he'd been knocking on her door! And he'd enquired about Lucy with that girl in the opposite flat, which wouldn't look good for him.

'Did you know she was in Portsmouth?'

Horton didn't care for the way Uckfield was eying him. Quickly he ran through the answer in his head, lie or tell the truth? There was no choice. 'Yes.'

Uckfield drew him further away from flapping ears. 'Who else knows?'

'Haven't got a clue. Jarrett, I expect.' He saw Uckfield frown.

'You know what I mean.'

'*I* haven't told anyone.' It wasn't a lie.

'How did you find out?'

'Does it matter?' He certainly wasn't going to drag Cantelli into this.

'It does if you have anything to do with this,' Uckfield snapped.

Horton tensed. 'That's twice you've accused me of being involved with a murder, Steve. What is it? Don't you trust me anymore?' He saw that he had unsettled Uckfield. The prospects of promotion were making the DCI edgy.

'It's not that.'

Horton remained silent forcing Uckfield to continue. 'You're too close to this one, Andy. I'll deal with it.'

He didn't like it but it was as he had expected. 'Then you'd better know what Jane Staveley told me.' Horton relayed the information about the party in the tower organised by Alpha One. 'Lucy must have seen the killer. We've got to find out where Thurlow's boat went that night. Jarrett's boat is moored opposite Thurlow's. Jarrett told me he went out that Friday afternoon but came back before the fog rolled in. He could have seen Thurlow or at least heard the *Free Spirit* leave the marina.'

'You've questioned Jarrett?' Uckfield's surprise swiftly changed to anger.

Horton couldn't help that. 'He was on his boat when I went to check out where the *Free Spirit* was berthed.' Should he tell the rest? How would Steve take it? It was time to find out. He couldn't hold back indefinitely and he certainly had enough for Uckfield to start an investigation.

He said, 'Jane also told me that someone high up was involved in framing me. It has to be either Reine or Superintendent Underwood. Neither of them stood by me.'

'Do you realise what you're saying?' Uckfield looked anxious.

Horton could understand that. 'Yes. Corruption at a high level.'

'But why?'

'Perhaps one of them likes a bit on the side or is being well paid to turn a blind eye. Steve, it has to be one of them and my money's on Reine.'

'No, I can't believe it.'

'Someone is trying to kill me. They tried to set my boat alight with me on it.'

'My God!'

'I think it was Jarrett or one of his cronies. I've been going through Culven's files. He was Jarrett's solicitor. I think Culven was money laundering for Jarrett's illegal pornography operation. We've got to investigate.'

Uckfield was looking very uncomfortable and Horton knew the reason why. Tomorrow was his promotion interview. Uckfield couldn't afford to rock the boat until after that. Horton would have let it lie until then, but he wasn't sure if Jarrett would let him live that long.

'We've got to take it higher, Steve.'

After a moment Uckfield said, 'OK, but not before I've spoken to Reg. No, listen, Andy. Let me have a quiet word in Reg's ear, sound him out. I'll take his advice.'

Horton wasn't altogether sure that talking to the Chief Constable was the right thing to do but on the other hand it made sense. He could authorise a full enquiry.

'When?'

'Tonight.'

'You'll have to let Melissa Thurlow go. Lucy's death puts her in the clear.'

'If it is connected and we don't know that for certain. Have you had any joy tracing this biographer?'

'Not yet.'

'Don't you think you might be barking up the wrong tree?'

'No.'

'Then get back to the station and see if you can find this mysterious non-existent author.'

'I could talk to the manager at Horsea Marina and get the names and addresses of berth holders on Thurlow's pontoon.'

'I'll apply for some extra officers first and then we'll get a team in there. You coordinate things back at the incident room. I'll hold a briefing at four o'clock.'

And that's it, thought Horton? Shoved aside again. He left, angry at Uckfield's attitude. A car dropped him back at the station where he found Cantelli at his desk. The sergeant's beaming face told him his family crisis was over.

'I take it Ellen has told you where she was and what was troubling her.'

'Yes. Sorry about being late this morning but Ellen decided to leave home. I went looking for her. She didn't get very far only to Isabella's, thank the Lord.'

Horton sat down opposite Cantelli. His mind only on half of what Cantelli was saying, the other half running through the facts of the case.

'She *did* go to a party with Sophie and Jaz. Not the one in Hemmings Road.'

'That was worrying you?'

'Yes. Kate Somerfield told me the kids were barely sixteen. It got me thinking. Anyway this party was in Milton. Ellen drank too much, some boy started pawing her and she didn't like it. Someone gave her ecstasy. I thought I was going to have a seizure right in the middle of Isabella's café when she told me. She didn't take it but slipped it into her pocket and came home and all I could do was ball her out.'

'Don't be so hard on yourself. What happened to the ecstasy?'

'She flushed it down the loo at home.'

'Best place for it.'

'Amen to that,' Cantelli said with feeling, then, 'Now tell me about Lucy. I've just heard the news.'

'She must have been dead when I was knocking on her door last night. I swear I had nothing to do with her death.'

'I know that,' Cantelli answered, dismissively. 'But who did? We've drawn a blank so far with anyone connected with Randall Simpson.'

Horton had been so sure he'd been on the right lines. Was every avenue of this investigation going to end up like this — going nowhere?

'I don't suppose there's much left from Culven's car?'

'It's being examined but I wouldn't hold your breath.'

'And we still haven't traced that tender.'

Cantelli shook his head.

'OK, bring me everything we've got on the two murders, both Culven and Thurlow. I'm going to go through every statement, and don't say the computer's already done that. *I* want to do it. You'd better check in with the incident room and help with Lucy's murder.'

Horton wondered how Uckfield was getting on. How soon would they know he had been at the scene? What had Phil and his scene-of-crime officers discovered? When was the post mortem being conducted? It was three p.m. when he called the mortuary.

'She was strangled,' Doctor Clayton told him. 'With a tie, or something similar, a piece of material anyway. Time of death about seven p.m. last night. There is no evidence of sexual intercourse or that she put up a struggle.'

'Does it fit the pattern of the other killings?'

'Apart from the sexual element, yes.'

He called the office at Horsea Marina and then headed along to the incident room. It was buzzing with activity. Officers from other stations and divisions had been drafted in. He crossed to Cantelli.

'Anything?'

'Phil Taylor says the room has been wiped clean.'

So, thought Horton, no DNA and no fingerprints. 'Where's the DCI?'

'With the Super.'

'If he asks where I am, you don't know.'

'I don't.'

'Fine.' He'd miss the briefing but that couldn't be helped. He didn't fancy standing around listening to others without leading the investigation, or at least being involved himself. He'd get a roasting from Uckfield but so be it.

Ten minutes later he was in the Horsea Marina office. The manager said he would be happy to supply a list of names and addresses and then showed him into the lock-master's control room.

Whereas the previous lockmaster he'd interviewed had been a barrel of a man and working on nights, this one was his opposite: lean and anxious with a hooked nose and sharp watery eyes. He'd been working on the day shift on the Friday Thurlow had disappeared and must also have seen Jarrett return.

'*Sunray*, yes. Came through about five o'clock,' the lockmaster said.

'Was Mr Jarrett alone?'

'No, had a couple of fellows with him.'

'Anyone you know?'

The lockmaster shook his head. 'Never seen them before.'

'And did he go out again?'

The lockmaster looked at him as if he had a screw loose. 'No. If I remember it was very foggy that night. Anyone would be mad to go out in that. Though they do. Or at least the *Free Spirit* did. Mr Thurlow's boat.'

Horton's heart skipped a beat. This he hadn't bargained for. He could hardly believe his luck. 'You saw it? I thought the other man was on duty that night. This is the Friday before last we're talking about?'

'Yes. Derek had gone for a quick leak. I happened to pop in. I'd left my glasses behind.'

A break! He could barely contain his excitement. 'Did you see who was piloting her?' Please don't say no, he silently prayed.

'It wasn't Mr Thurlow. I heard he's been killed, I suppose that's why you want to know.'

Horton tried to squeeze the impatience from his voice as he said, 'Can you describe this man?'

'Tall fellow, lean, looks fit.'

It couldn't be Calthorpe then.

'I've seen him go out with Mr Jarrett a few times.'

What! He hadn't expected that. Now his pulse was racing. 'Do you know his name?'

'No. Mr Jarrett will though.'

Won't he just. This was better than he had dared to hope. But it put paid to his theory about the murders being linked to Melissa Thurlow. Uckfield was right when he said he'd been barking up the wrong tree. This had nothing to do with framing Melissa Thurlow and everything to do with Jarrett's porn operation.

He tore down to Jarrett's pontoon but was disappointed to find his boat wasn't there. He returned to the station, his mind racing. He found Cantelli at his desk.

'Uckfield's been screaming for you.'

'I'm onto something, Barney.' Horton relayed what the lockmaster had said. 'In one of the statements a man reported seeing someone running along Ferry Road late on the Tuesday night of Culven's killing. I think it's the same man that took out Thurlow's boat. Tell Sergeant Trueman to check all the statements the night Thurlow was killed and alert the team working on questioning Lucy's neighbours.'

His phone rang and he was summoned to Uckfield's office.

He could see immediately by Steve's frozen expression that he knew he'd been to Lucy's flat. He didn't even have time to tell him about the breakthrough on the murder case.

Uckfield said, his voice terse, 'Why didn't you tell me you called on Lucy Richardson last night?'

Horton had been expecting it but he had hoped he'd have a little more time before Uckfield found out. He remained silent. There wasn't much he could say.

'You should have told me,' Uckfield snapped.

'I went there and there was no answer.'

Uckfield looked as though he didn't believe him. Horton was sickened by what he saw in Uckfield's eyes. 'I know I can't prove it. I didn't think I would have to, not to you, Steve.'

'It's not me you have to convince. Superintendent Reine wants to see you.'

Uckfield rose and they walked in a tense silence to Reine's office. Horton's heart sank to the pit of his stomach. This wasn't going to be good. Would it be another suspension?

Reine looked up as they entered. He was sitting behind his desk in uniform, his round shiny face solemn and perspiring in the stifling heat. Horton could see he'd get no help from Uckfield. Until Uckfield spoke to his father-in-law he was on his own.

Reine ran a hand over his balding head, removed his reading glasses and eyed Horton coldly. He didn't invite him to sit.

'Last night you called on Lucy Richardson. Why?'

Jane Staveley's words reverberated through his head. *Someone high up.* 'That's my business,' he said, stiffly.

'I don't think so, Inspector Horton,' Reine snapped. 'I think it is mine especially when someone known to you — shall we even say close to you — has been brutally murdered.'

'You can't seriously believe I have anything to do with her death?' He was damned if he was going to say 'sir.'

'She has done a great deal to harm you, Inspector. Maybe you didn't know your own strength? Maybe you wanted revenge for what she'd done to you?'

Oh clever. Jarrett had primed him well. 'That's rubbish!'

'Is it?'

Horton glared at him but said nothing. There was nothing he could say, not here to that man and not now.

'I am suspending you from duty until further notice.'

He'd guessed as much.

'I must also warn you that you will be formally cautioned and questioned in connection with Lucy's death,' Reine said coldly. 'We will need details of your movements both last night and this morning and these will need to be corroborated.'

He had to find a way out. He wasn't going to let them get him into an interview room, and then a cell, while they cooked up some cock and bull story and tried to fit him up for Lucy's murder.

'Your warrant card, Inspector.'

Horton reached inside his jacket pocket and placed the card on Reine's desk with a feeling he would never get it back again.

Reine crossed to the door where a decidedly uncomfortable looking Marsden hovered on the threshold.

'Escort Inspector Horton to the interview room and stay there with him until Internal Investigations arrive,' Reine instructed.

Horton held Uckfield's stare for a few moments before turning.

'Am I allowed to go back to my office to collect a couple of personal things?'

'The Super said not,' Marsden hesitated. 'What's going on, sir?'

But Cantelli appeared behind Marsden and said, 'I'll see the Inspector gets to the interview room, Jake.'

'But the Super—'

'I'm taking over from now.'

After a moment's hesitation Marsden nodded and walked off.

Cantelli pushed back the door of the social club and Horton followed him inside. Cantelli closed and locked the door behind them. The room was empty and they walked swiftly to the bar area.

'Reine thinks I killed her,' Horton said, as Cantelli lifted the counter flap and they made their way through to the small storeroom behind it.

'That's ridiculous.'

'I know, but I can't let Internal Investigations get hold of me, not yet anyway.' Horton looked at the fire exit.

'What are you going to do?'

'You don't need to know that, Barney. Look, I appreciate you helping me like this. You're already risking suspension when Reine finds out you've let me go.'

'Well I've been promising Charlotte I'd decorate the lounge for a long time now,' and he grinned. 'Come on.'

Horton could see Barney had made up his mind. He was rather glad to have him along. He pushed open the door. Stepping onto the fire escape he peered down. There was no one standing guard at the bottom of it. It came out into the car park. They reached Cantelli's car without being accosted.

'Where to?' Cantelli asked, stretching the seat belt around him.

Horton lifted a pile of Cantelli's children's drawings onto the back seat and said, 'Jarrett's boat.'

SIXTEEN

By the time they reached the marina the wind had risen and the halyards were slapping against the masts. The stifling heat had vanished and the fat rain had developed into lean, mean streaks. Horton thought he heard the faint rumble of thunder as they slipped onto the pontoon brushing past a man coming out.

Hurrying towards Jarrett's boat Horton could see that the cover was off which meant that Jarrett must be on board. He wondered why he hadn't covered over his precious yacht to protect it from the weather. As he climbed on board and dipped below into the cabin he saw the answer.

He cursed quietly and stepped aside. Jarrett was lying on his back, his eyes were staring up into nothing. There was blood around his mouth and a livid mark around his neck. Horton felt for the pulse in Jarrett's neck even though he knew there was no point. The body was still warm. He straightened up shaking his head at Cantelli who looked shocked and worried. Horton knew where this would leave him. They would try and pin Jarrett's murder on him along with Lucy's.

Cantelli said, 'Is it the same killer?'

'Looks like it.' Horton was unable to disguise the disappointment he felt. 'Chummy seems to go in for strangulation.'

'This doesn't make sense. Why kill Jarrett? What has he got to do with Melissa Thurlow?'

'Nothing. The murders have no connection with Melissa Thurlow. I was wrong.' Horton stepped back on deck under the protective cover of the spray hood. He could hear the rain beating against it and splattering on to the pristine deck. 'I didn't expect this. I should have done.' He tried to clear his brain. Think damn you, think.

'You'd better phone through and get the circus in.' He couldn't stick around here and wait for Uckfield. 'Can I borrow your car, Barney?'

Cantelli looked surprised. 'Where are you going?'

'Away from here, that's for sure.'

'I discovered the body with you,' Cantelli protested.

'By the time Uckfield and Reine are convinced of that it will be too late.' He wasn't prepared to tell Barney his suspicions about Reine being the someone 'high up' that Jane had mentioned. He didn't want Cantelli compromised, or at risk, any more than he already was. 'Tell them you were acting on a hunch coming out here. Don't mention me.'

'And if they ask me where my car is?'

'I'm sure you'll think of something. And try and trace that man we saw slipping off the pontoon as we came in. Did you get a look at him?'

Cantelli frowned. 'Not a proper one, sorry.'

Neither had Horton, though he felt there was something familiar about him. 'I'll call you.'

Horton climbed into Cantelli's car. Four people dead — Culven, Thurlow, Lucy and now Jarrett — and no nearer to finding the killer. There had to be something he'd overlooked. Could the lockmaster give a better description? Had anyone else seen and recognised this man on Thurlow's boat? Oh they'd find out, once they'd questioned the marina staff and berth holders but how long would that take and where would he be then? Still suspended — again.

He slid the driver's seat back to accommodate his longer legs but it got stuck. He reached underneath to find a child's drawing book stuffed in the space. He grabbed it and made to throw it on the back seat when his hand froze. He glanced down at the drawings he'd already thrown there. Rapidly he examined them and then the drawings in the book, his heart going like the clappers. He sat back and thought. Cantelli's drawings on his notice board, the twins writing underneath them and on these drawings . . . Melissa Thurlow's belief that she had an illegitimate brother or sister. Could it be a twin brother or sister? There were the love letters to Culven that Melissa had denied writing and yet were in an identical hand.

He stared at the drawings illuminated in a flash of lightning, you couldn't tell the difference between the Cantelli twins writing. He recalled the lockmaster's description: a lean fit man — an athlete, a runner.

He swung the car out of Horsea Marina. His heart was still racing. The photographs on the wall of Thurlow's boardroom had shown a man with a marathon medal and a group of disabled children. The business was losing money but Calthorpe had seemed unaware of it. Culven's files had mentioned redundancies. Why hadn't he seen the likeness before? Oh yes, Melissa did have a twin and that twin was Graham Parnham. But how could it be? His alibi confirmed he'd been in France. Horton thought it time he questioned him more closely. He recalled his address from the statement he had made and headed for the coastal village of Emsworth.

Parnham's house was in darkness and despite ringing the bell and knocking several times Horton knew he wasn't there. Where could he have gone? If he was right — though as yet there was no evidence to say he was — this was a man who had killed three people, four if he was responsible for Jarrett's death, but Horton wasn't sure about that. This was a man who would kill again to achieve his goal, which was . . . He wasn't sure exactly what that was, only that it was connected to Melissa Thurlow and that if he was right about Parnham, then there was only one place Parnham would have gone.

The lightning was flashing across the sky like an erratic searchlight and the thunder booming like a hundred canons by the time Horton reached Briarly House. It was in darkness. Perhaps Melissa had gone to stay with friends?

He stepped back and looked up at the window. Then he walked around to the back of the house searching for the best way to enter. He pushed against the conservatory door. It opened.

Gingerly he crept through the kitchen, his ears straining for the slightest of sounds but all he could hear was the thunder. From his previous visits he knew the house wasn't alarmed.

He negotiated the hall, knocking his shin on the corner of a table and cursing softly under his breath. Swiftly, but stealthily, he searched the rooms on the ground floor but found nothing and no one.

Upstairs he stood in the pitch black and strained his ears but heard only the wind and rain. A growing sense of anxiety was beginning to creep up his spine. Something wasn't quite right. He felt uneasy. This house wasn't empty. He'd known from the moment he had stepped over the threshold, only he'd chosen to ignore his instinct. Now his pulse quickened and he tried to still his pounding heart as he eased his way along the landing. Carefully and slowly, he pushed back a door to a bedroom, nothing, then another into the bathroom. Deserted.

He made his way down the passageway to the room at the end. Gingerly, with his fingertips, he pushed open the door. Slowly it swung wide.

She was lying on the bed, much as Lucy Richardson had been, but Melissa Thurlow was face down and wearing a green dressing gown. An empty bottle of pills and an empty whisky bottle lay by her side on the floor. Her arm was hanging over the edge of the bed where she had let it fall.

Swiftly he crossed to the bed believing her to be dead but when he pressed his fingers against her neck he felt a pulse. Thank God. He lifted the telephone, but something struck him violently on the side of the head, and he fell to the floor. Before he even had a chance to recover a gun was thrust at his temple.

'Over there,' a voice commanded.

He obeyed. His head was muggy from the blow. He felt his arms being wrenched behind him while his brain said, resist, fight back, but that gun was at his head. Whatever bound him was made of material. The bonds were tightened.

'Up.'

He struggled up.

'Turn around.'

He did so knowing who he would be facing. He'd recognised the voice.

Parnham said, 'I don't mind shooting you here if I have to, so don't try anything, Inspector.'

Slowly Horton's mind began to clear. 'Let me call an ambulance,' he said, 'She's still alive.'

'All the more reason not to call one.'

Was he going to have to stand here and watch Melissa slowly die while this man gloated?

Parnham's eyes flickered to Melissa for a moment but almost instantly came back up again and focused on Horton before he had a chance to take advantage of it. He must think of a way to overpower Parnham and get help for Melissa before it was too late. But he was staring at a ruthless, unbalanced and complex personality. If Melissa died, that would make four deaths this man had committed. Parnham wasn't responsible for Jarrett's because Horton now knew who the man slipping off the pontoon had been. But what good was that if he didn't get out of here? Parnham wouldn't hesitate to kill him, but to do so here would be a mistake. He would need to get him away from Briarly House and then Horton would have to take his chance. But it might be too late for Melissa.

He said, 'You're going to stand there and let your twin sister die?'

'You know, then.' Parnham looked disappointed. A flicker of annoyance showed behind the eyes, this time without their spectacles. Horton could see the likeness between them more strongly. He cursed himself for not spotting it sooner, but Parnham's spectacles, and the light shining off them from Thurlow's office window, had deceived him. He remembered how Parnham had removed his spectacles and polished them, a gesture, Horton now guessed, designed to taunt him.

Parnham continued, 'She had nothing but luxury and comfort all her life. She never had to work and scrimp and save like me.'

'You killed her because of that!' goaded Horton. The longer he kept him talking the more chance he had of getting out of this alive.

'Why not? I couldn't get my revenge on my stupid, selfish mother. And besides Roger was going to make me redundant. How could I get another position at my age? Especially one so lucrative.'

'You were taking money out of the company.'

'I was drawing the director's pay I was entitled to.'

'And you didn't think that was putting pressure on the business and hence your proposed redundancy?' Horton scoffed.

Parnham scowled. 'The business would have been fine if Roger and Charles hadn't been so greedy, but then when you're keeping a mistress as Roger was, and living an expensive lifestyle as Charles was then you have expenses. Why should I be the one to suffer because of his greedy incompetence?'

'You overheard Thurlow and Culven talking about the redundancies in the yacht club on that Friday?'

A sharp flash of lightning lit the room illuminating Parnham's face for a moment. Almost instantly it was followed by a deafening crack of thunder, which shook the house and rattled the thin windowpanes. Parnham didn't even flinch. It was as though he were living in an existence of his own, totally oblivious of the storm raging around him. Horton could hear the wind chasing itself around the house and the mean rain lashing against the windows with such ferocity that he thought the panes might shatter.

Parnham said, 'I heard Roger arranging the meeting with Culven and knew they were up to something. The company has corporate membership of the yacht club so I simply went there before Roger and waited. They couldn't see me from where they were sitting.'

Horton had to raise his voice to be heard above the storm. 'So you planned your revenge?'

'I'd planned that a long time ago. I just had to speed things up a bit.'

'Does Melissa know you're her twin?' Horton wondered if she was still alive. He prayed she was.

'She does now. Or rather she did before she tragically took her own life.' The gun wavered for a second. 'I told her. I think I'll tell you before you die in tragic circumstances. A drowning accident might be suitable.'

'Don't bother. I know most of it. Your mother took Melissa out of Barnardo's when she met Randall Simpson because he had admitted to her he couldn't have children. You'd already been adopted.'

'Yes by Agnes and Bert Parnham. But it wasn't an official adoption. My mother was billeted with them during the war. When she got pregnant after the war, she returned to stay with them, handing me over to the Parnhams as soon as I was born and putting Melissa into Barnardo's. I was condemned to spend my childhood and youth growing up in poverty while she had everything.'

Horton doubted Parnham's upbringing had been as bleak as that but it had been poor compared to Melissa. 'When did you find out about Melissa?' Again the flash of lightning and roar of thunder. Horton prayed they'd be struck by a thunderbolt, if it didn't kill them it might give him a chance of escape.

Parnham was saying calmly and evenly, 'I found a letter when my adoptive mother died just over ten years ago. It was from my birth mother crowing about her new life. It gave me enough information about Randall Simpson to identify him and track down Melissa.'

'The false biography.'

'I see you have been busy.'

'But why kill the others? Roger Thurlow, all right, I can see your twisted reasoning there, you wanted the blame to fall on Melissa. But why kill Culven and Lucy Richardson?'

'Oh I didn't intend to kill the girl,' he said airily, 'She brought it on herself really. I thought she might have seen me dump Roger in the tower. Still, she was only a tart.'

Horton tensed and his fists curled behind his back, but what good was that when he couldn't strike out.

Parnham smiled. 'Roger was my intended victim all along. By killing him and framing Melissa I would destroy her comfortable life. I wanted her to know what it felt like to be an outsider. I wanted her to experience the sensation of disintegration. I wanted her to feel shame and disgrace, as I had felt it. Then finally to feel fear, just as I've felt fear all my life, the fear of failing and poverty. She pleaded with me in the end, you know. Said she'd give me everything and anything I wanted, this house even, but then I'm going to get this anyway, as her only blood relative, so why should I let her live?'

Parnham needed to talk, to explain. If he got out of this alive Horton wanted Parnham to as well. He needed him to tell his story. He moved back towards the window just a fraction hoping that Parnham wouldn't notice.

Horton said, 'And France? Your alibi?'

'Clever that, wasn't it? I was in France as no doubt you and the good sergeant checked. But instead of taking the ferry like I told you, I took the high speed catamaran, the first one on Saturday morning to Cherbourg. It leaves Portsmouth at 5.30 a.m. and gets in at Cherbourg at 8.15 a.m. I had a hire car waiting at Cherbourg and drove to St Malo in time to go to the bakers.'

'Then you came back by the high speed on Tuesday in time to kill Culven and not the ferry which you were booked on to on the Wednesday.'

'Yes. As I was leaving the ferry port on foot I saw the tart who had been in the tower walking down to the railway station. I picked her up and we went back to her place where I stayed for most of the day.'

The gun wavered a bit but not enough for Horton to attempt anything especially with his hands tied behind his back. 'How did you kill Roger Thurlow?'

'On Friday I went after Roger to his boat. By the time I got there he was asleep.'

'Unconscious actually. Melissa had drugged his water. She wanted him dead. You did her a favour.' Horton could see Parnham didn't like that much.

After a moment Parnham continued. 'I wanted to tell him why he had to die, but you can't look a gift horse in the mouth, can you? So I put a plastic bag over his head and held it there until he died.'

What did the man want? Praise? Horton's expression remained impassive but all the time, behind the mask, he was desperately seeking a way out. The gun was still aimed at his head with a steady hand. Parnham's gaze never wavered from him.

'It was foggy of course, ideal conditions. I hadn't really planned for that,' he said, as if he could have done so if he wished. 'I took the *Free Spirit* through the lock on free flow and motored to Emsworth where I picked up a buoy.'

Much as Horton had guessed. 'And the clothes? Did Thurlow really dress up in women's clothes?'

Parnham laughed. 'No, of course he didn't. I brought the clothes with me. I picked them up in a charity shop. I undressed and re-dressed Roger. Have you ever tried to dress someone who's dead, Inspector? No? Well I don't recommend it. It is extremely difficult. I put him in the tender and motored near to the shore and then dragged the tender with Roger in it up the tower and dumped him.'

Was Melissa still alive? Horton agonised, but he couldn't stop Parnham now.

'It was just after midnight. I waited for a while. Saw a couple of girls come out of the track, then two men. They were very drunk, or drugged. I recognized Culven. When it was quiet, I dumped Roger inside but the girl came back. I couldn't be sure she hadn't seen me so she had to die. Then

I motored back to the shore at Emsworth, where I left the tender and ran home.'

Behind Horton was a window but he was on the second floor. He wouldn't have time to get out of it before Parnham pulled that trigger and besides he'd probably break his neck landing on the gravel drive beneath him.

'Now, I think it's time we made a move, Inspector. She must be dead by now.' Parnham prodded him towards the door.

Perhaps he could throw himself down the stairs? But no, that would only make Parnham fire the gun at him and he might end up breaking his leg, or his neck.

'How did you lure Culven to his death?' he asked, desperate to keep him talking until he could find a way out of this.

'Easy. On Tuesday evening I called Culven and asked him to meet me in the car park at Eastney. He did. He would have done anything for me by then.'

'You were lovers?'

'He was infatuated with me. I knew all about his little fetish and Alpha One.'

'What about Alpha One?' Horton stopped.

'I think you already know. Isn't that why you were suspended? Lucy told me all about it.'

'She told you who framed me?' His heart quickened.

'Oh yes. You'd like to know of course.'

Horton knew Parnham was playing with him.

'Maybe I'll tell you before I kill you. I suppose it would be a kindness. Move on, Inspector.' He jabbed the gun in Horton's back and continued, 'Of course Jarrett's smuggling pornography.'

'How do you know?'

'Lucy told me, although she didn't really need to. I've been out with Jarrett several times. I know a great deal about Colin Jarrett. It could come in useful.'

'I doubt it, he's dead.'

Parnham halted for a moment. 'Is he?'

'You didn't kill him?'

'No. Pity. Still to get back to Culven.' He prodded the gun in Horton's back and urged him forward. 'We went down onto the beach; it was dark and foggy. I was walking behind him, throwing stones into the sea like you do, and then I strangled him. He wasn't a very strong man. I dragged him along the beach so he wouldn't be washed out to sea and then I stripped him and bundled his clothes up and put them in the boot of his Mercedes. I then drove it to Horsea Marina where I planted the letters in his house. I could use him to really make Melissa suffer. I guessed the police would arrest her. Quite a good idea, don't you think? Then I took the car to Stansted Woods and flashed it up. I ran back to Emsworth from there, got in the tender and took the *Free Spirit* out. I set it adrift after getting into the tender and motored it round to Eastney Lake where I left it. After that I jogged back to Lucy's flat, where I stayed until I headed to the ferry port to coincide with the time of my ferry, and took a taxi home, carrying the bag I'd previously left at Lucy's. Quite a good bit of improvisation that, wouldn't you say?'

'So there was no affair between Melissa and Culven?'

'None whatsoever. The letters were clever, weren't they? Twins, you see, sometimes have identical handwriting. I'd managed to get a sample of her writing all those years ago from the house, but I needn't have bothered. It was the same as mine. It confirmed what I already knew, that we were related.'

They were in front of the garage. Horton was soaked to the skin. The rain was lashing against him, dripping off his ears and his nose.

'Don't you think it's a very capable revenge, Inspector?'

'You won't get her money. You'll be arrested for murder by then.'

'Oh but I won't. There's only you who knows the truth and you won't be around for much longer.'

Parnham opened the boot of Melissa's Ford. Horton wondered if he could swing round and headbutt Parnham, or at least ram his head into his belly and wound him. But Parnham must have sensed his thoughts because before Horton had the chance, something came down violently on the back of his head and the blackness swallowed him up.

SEVENTEEN

He was moving slowly and jerkily. With each violent tug, pain screamed through his body. Horton could hear grunting. He didn't think it was coming from him, but it could have been. Someone was pounding on his head as if they'd found a new substitute for a drum and he was being hauled along the ground. He was drenched from the rain that was beating against his battered body, and at any moment, he thought the scream inside his head might erupt through his mouth and at the same time spill the contents of his stomach. He fought to control the pain and nausea, as he realised that he was encased in something.

He tried to get his bearings and some semblance of clear thinking into his befuddled mind, but along with the loss of one of his senses came the acuteness of another. He sniffed. Beyond the smell of the sea he could smell dog. He was wrapped in something, a blanket? What had happened to Bellman? Where was he? Perhaps he was still with the dog handler? Perhaps Parnham had killed him too, because by now Melissa must be dead.

The dragging and grunting continued. Where had Parnham brought him? What was he going to do with him? How could he get away? He pushed the drum out of his head and urged his sluggish mind to start thinking of a way out of this. The ground scraped at the blanket and tore into him. His body twisted and turned with the movement. Parnham was pulling him.

He tried to move his legs but they were tied, as were his hands, behind his back. Parnham had mentioned a drowning accident but he would have to untie him before throwing him into the sea if he wanted it to look like suicide. To untie him meant he'd have to lean over and that might be the only chance Horton would get before Parnham knocked him unconscious again.

He struggled against his bonds. He was soaked from the rain. What would they say when his body was washed up along the south coast: that he had committed suicide rather than face the disgrace of a suspension? That he couldn't face the fact that he'd killed Lucy Richardson and Colin Jarrett? Melissa would be dead and Uckfield and others would believe she had taken her own life after killing her husband and lover. Her twin brother would be found and inherit the estate. How nice and tidy. What an easy way out for them. And Emma would grow up believing her father to be both a pervert and a murderer. He wouldn't have it, he *couldn't*. The thought filled him with a fury so fierce that it blotted out any pain he was feeling and he struggled against the bonds.

There would be a moment when Parnham would reach the shore. It was coming now, the hard ground gave way to the shingle and stones, the shells were jarring against him and cutting through the blanket into his flesh. He could hear the waves crashing onto the shore, sucking the stones back as they receded and then tossing them again onto the beach. Parnham would be exhausted. He was strong to have hauled him the short distance to the shore but the effort must have weakened him.

Horton tensed his aching body. He had to marshal his strength. There would be a split second when Parnham would stop, then he would need to untie the blanket and him. It was a risk, a big one, a gigantic gamble that could cost him his life but he decided it might be the only one he had.

He let his body go limp as if unconscious. It took all the nerve he could muster. He felt the sea wash against his face, filling his eyes, his mouth, his nose. He tasted the salt and fought to stop himself from choking. The thunder crashed around them.

Parnham was panting heavily. Horton held his breath and remained absolutely still as the sea washed over him and out again. After what seemed like hours, but could only have been a few seconds, Parnham began to unwind whatever it was he had wrapped around him to keep the blanket in place. Horton kept his eyes closed and his head loose as he felt Parnham's breath on his face. Parnham manhandled him over onto his stomach. Horton's face was pressed into the seabed. His breath coming fast. Parnham undid the bonds that tied his feet and then his hands. Then he turned him over so that he was lying on his back. One satisfied grunt told Horton that Parnham had straightened up and now was his chance. It seemed to be agonisingly slow. He was beginning to feel as if he had spent his whole life in this wretched state. His nerves were stretched to breaking point. His head was throbbing so much that he thought it might explode. With a great cry, totally blind and with all the force he could muster he sprang up and charged at Parnham.

He hit Parnham's unprepared stomach and the two men crashed down into the sea. Horton's battered body rolled over. He heard himself cry out, hardly recognising his own voice. He could hear Parnham's cries against the splashing of the water and the crashing of the thunder. He saw his face in the streak of lightning, startled and manic.

He stumbled up, but Parnham came charging at him, wielding a large stone retrieved from the seabed. Horton rolled out of his reach but it wasn't far enough. It caught a glancing blow on his shoulder and he howled in pain. He knew he had to get away before it would come crashing down again. Summoning his remaining energy, he leapt to his feet. To give himself time, he ran away from Parnham as fast as the large stones on the beach would allow him; his body pitching forward, stumbling.

Parnham was running after him. Horton would have only seconds to pick up something, turn and bring it down on Parnham's head. He'd underestimated Parnham's fitness. The man's strength surprised him. Parnham pushed him back into the sea, his face ugly with anger, his eyes cold and glaringly mad.

Horton took in a mouthful of salty water, making him choke and his stomach heave. Parnham, seizing his advantage, grabbed hold of his head and forced it under. Horton gasped and let in more seawater. He went down. His fingers reached out for something, anything: a weapon he could use to strike out against the man possessed and intent on drowning him.

His breathing was growing shallower. The world was growing darker. He was taking in too much water. He was going to die without ever seeing Emma again. He *couldn't* die. He wouldn't let it happen. His body was going slack. Parnham's grip was getting tighter. Parnham's hand was on his head forcing him down and holding him down. He knew he would have to make one last supreme effort and with that he would either live or die.

Mustering every ounce of strength and every fibre of will-power, he stretched out his fingers. It curled around something. He had no idea what it was and he was beyond caring, only that what he held in his hand must save his life. With energy that he dragged up from somewhere deep inside him, and sensing Parnham's loosening his grip through lack of resistance, Horton pushed himself to the surface. Reaching out, he struck Parnham across the face with the long, metal bar. There was a crash of bone and the sound of tearing flesh. Parnham screamed, staggered back, his hands to his bloodied head and face. Horton didn't wait, he crashed his fist into Parnham's face and the man splashed back into the sea and his body went limp.

Horton reached out for Parnham's shirt, grabbed it and pulled him up. He hit him again and again. And then because he wanted to go on hitting him, finally forced himself to stop. Parnham was unconscious.

Horton hauled him up the shore and crashed down onto the beach gasping for breath as the sea washed around his aching body. His head pounded violently. His lungs were full of seawater. He retched and was sick on the stones.

A voice came out of the darkness, startling him. 'Feeling better now?'

Horton stiffened. Instinctively he knew it meant trouble. This wasn't some concerned passer-by. He looked up already knowing who he was going to see.

'Thoughtful of Parnham to leave his gun in the car,' Tom Maddox said, pointing it at Horton. 'Is he dead?'

'No.'

'Pity. I'll have to do it for you.'

This was who Lucy meant when she had told Jane that someone 'high up' had paid her. It wasn't someone in the police force but in import control.

Horton eased his body into a more upright position. It was difficult to see Maddox's expression but he didn't doubt his intentions. God! He'd just escaped from one lunatic only to face another. This time he wasn't sure if he had the strength, both physical and mental, to deal with it. But he had to live to tell his story. Fatigue had drained him but his instinct for survival was still strong. The need to know the truth was sending fresh adrenalin pumping through his pain-racked body and clearing his head.

He said, 'Why would you want to kill Parnham?'

'Why do you think?'

'He knows you're smuggling pornography.' Hadn't Parnham hinted as much? 'Did Jarrett tell him?'

'Jarrett or Culven. Does it matter?'

'Culven was money laundering for the operation and you were the brains behind it all. It was you I saw leaving the pontoon.' Horton's mind grappled for a way out of this. The overhanging branches from the trees were protecting him and Maddox from the worst of the rain. The lightning had lessened and the thunder was now only a distant rumble. If he couldn't see Maddox clearly then perhaps Maddox couldn't see him. Gently he shifted position.

Maddox said, 'I thought you might have recognised me, so I followed you. I was hoping Parnham would do my job for me.'

Slowly Horton stretched out his left arm, his fingers exploring the ground for a possible weapon. 'But why kill Jarrett? Hasn't that ruined your nice little earner?'

'It was over anyway. You saw to that. I thought we'd got rid of you but you kept coming back like a boomerang. Jarrett was too much of a risk. You would have got him to talk, eventually. Anyway it was good while it lasted.'

Horton's hand connected with a piece of wood. His fingers curled around it. 'How did you do it, Maddox?' Got it. He tightened his grip. Maddox hadn't seen.

'You probably know.'

Horton did. 'Jarrett recruited men who owned boats and used them to ferry the pornography from France and Spain across the Channel. Jarrett gave you the name of the boats and you made sure they weren't stopped and searched, or if they were then nothing was found. And Parnham was in it with Jarrett.'

Horton turned to look at the inert figure of Parnham beside him knowing that Maddox would instinctively do the same. He did and in that split second, Horton sprang up and struck Maddox a resounding blow across the head with the branch. The gun went off. Throwing himself at Maddox, Horton wrestled him to the ground and the gun spun away. Grabbing Maddox by the jacket, Horton lifted his head and bashed it against the stones not once but three times until the man's body went limp. Horton slumped down onto the stones and let out a long exhalation of breath. No time to relax though. He had to get moving. He searched for the gun, found it, and pocketed it in his sodden jacket. Then he checked that both men were still unconscious and set off for the telephone box on the corner of Warlingham Lane.

EIGHTEEN

Friday

The thunderstorm had cleared the air and ushered in a fresh, bright day. There were white things in the sky that, if Horton remembered correctly, were called clouds. He could see them through the window of the hospital accident and emergency ward. His cuts had been stitched, his arm was in a sling, his shoulder aching like mad but nothing was broken, thank goodness. He didn't need the doctor to tell him he'd had a lucky escape, he knew that.

The cubicle curtains opened and Uckfield bounded in like a puppy that had been given a new bone. Horton tensed. He couldn't forget the look on Uckfield's face at that interview with Reine, nor the fact that he hadn't uttered one word in support of him.

'How's Melissa?' Horton asked.

'Recovering. She asked for Bellman.'

Horton smiled to himself. She hadn't collected Bellman from Dave the Dog immediately on her release, which was a stroke of luck for Parnham at the time, but not for Melissa. Now it had swung the other way.

'Good work, Andy.'

'Yeah, just in the nick of time too. When's the interview?'

If Uckfield heard the sarcasm in Horton's voice he didn't show it. 'I'm on my way there now. If I get the job, you'll be on my team.'

'And Sergeant Cantelli?'

'I'll have to see.'

'He came up with the twin theory.' Horton held Uckfield's gaze. It wasn't strictly true, but if it hadn't been for those drawings then things would have turned out very differently. And it was Cantelli that he had to thank for having enough faith in him to get him out of the station.

Uckfield said, 'I thought you'd like to know that Maddox has admitted to getting Lucy to lie about you raping her and Parnham is also crowing over his crimes like a cockerel in a henhouse. It's just a case of tying up the loose ends now.'

Horton guessed that Maddox must also have planted that cigarette lighter on his boat and tried to fry him alive. Had it been Jarrett in that car waiting to speed Maddox away after that incident? And had it been Jarrett who had knocked him off his bike? Probably. He'd find out soon enough.

Uckfield said, 'Oh, I nearly forgot. Thought you might like this back.'

Horton looked at the warrant card in Uckfield's hand. 'And Operation Extra?'

'The slate is wiped clean, Andy.'

'I was right then.'

'You were right.'

After all this time Horton had heard what he had been praying for. Yet, he hesitated. Should he take the warrant card? Did he want to stay in the force?

His body screamed with fatigue. His head was pounding but the raging, revengeful monster inside him had gone. As he'd listened to Parnham crowing over his revenge he had realised how destructive an emotion it was not only for Parnham but for the others around him who had paid with their lives: Thurlow, Culven and Lucy. With the act of smashing his fist into Parnham's face it was as though he had vent his own fury. He knew what he wanted now. He reached out his hand and took the card.

After Uckfield had left, Horton lay back on the pillow and closed his eyes. Would he now get to see Emma? Would he once again hold her in his arms, hear her voice and see her smile? His heart ached far more than his shoulder.

'It's all right for some.'

Horton opened his eyes to see Cantelli's slight figure and drawn face. The sergeant's dark eyes were ringed with fatigue. Horton knew that he and the team had been up all night checking statements and alibis, contacting the French police and ferry companies. Soon, they would delve deeply into the affairs of Bert and Agnes Parnham and complete the picture.

Horton said, 'You look as though you should be in here instead of me.'

Cantelli gave a tired smile. 'How did you know Maddox killed Jarrett?'

'It wasn't until I saw Parnham at Briarly House and he wasn't wearing his glasses that it clicked. Parnham must have been wearing contact lenses. When we saw that man leaving the pontoon, before we discovered Jarrett's body, he looked familiar but I couldn't think why. Maddox wasn't wearing his glasses. People can look quite different when you see them without their specs. Our arrival at Jarrett's boat was bad timing for Maddox but good for us.'

'Well, you're in the clear now, Andy. With two results in one night the Super will probably give you the key to his executive toilet. You're lucky to be alive though.'

'It was thinking of Emma that gave me the strength. I didn't want her to grow up believing I'd killed myself and that I was a murderer.'

And Catherine — was there still a chance for them? Did he *want* there to be a chance anymore? He didn't know.

Cantelli broke through his thoughts. 'You know you can't lie there all day.'

'Barney, I've been injured.'

'A few cuts and bruises that's all. That nice looking doctor, the one with those soulful eyes and legs that you could die for, said you were fine. I've brought you some clean clothes.'

'What's your hurry?'

'We're an officer down and the work's been piling up since we've been handling this case.'

Horton hauled himself up and squinted up at Cantelli. He knew what Cantelli was doing. 'I haven't fallen off a horse,' he muttered, but Cantelli was right, picking up the pieces of your life and getting on with it *was* the only option when you'd been betrayed and rejected. What else could you do except roll over and give in? And that was something he could never do.

Cantelli raised his dark bushy eyebrows and shrugged as only someone with Latin blood can. It warmed Horton's heart. Whatever Uckfield said and offered, Horton knew that if Cantelli wasn't going to be on the team, then he wouldn't want to be either.

He swung his legs over the side of the bed. 'Well, don't just stand there, sergeant, help me get dressed. We've got some villains to catch.'

THE END

ALSO BY PAULINE ROWSON

THE SOLENT MURDER MYSTERIES
Book 1: THE PORTSMOUTH MURDERS

Join the Joffe Books mailing list to be the first to hear about the next book in the series.

Thank you for reading this book.

If you enjoyed it please leave feedback on Amazon or Goodreads, and if there is anything we missed or you have a question about, then please get in touch. We appreciate you choosing our book.

Founded in 2014 in Shoreditch, London, we at Joffe Books pride ourselves on our history of innovative publishing. We were thrilled to be shortlisted for Independent Publisher of the Year at the British Book Awards.

www.joffebooks.com

We're very grateful to eagle-eyed readers who take the time to contact us. Please send any errors you find to corrections@joffebooks.com. We'll get them fixed ASAP.

Printed in Great Britain
by Amazon

46936060R00111